# RACHEL

## AMISH YOUNG LOVE

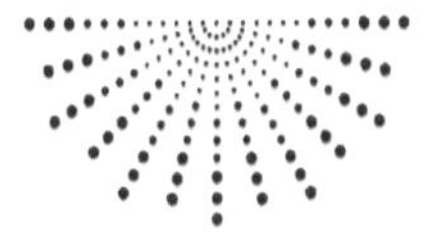

SARAH MILLER

IRENE GLICK

SWEETBOOKHUB.COM

# CHAPTER ONE

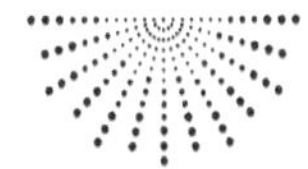

FAITH'S CREEK, PENNSYLVANIA.

"The entire farm?" Abel Amsbary said, staring at his wife, Victoria in disbelief.

"That's what Sarah Beiler told me," she replied, raising her eyebrows. "She said they'd come down from Ohio for one look and said yes straight away to old Willett Peachey. He wasn't going to say no to cash in hand." She chuckled. "He's happy, they're happy, and Clearfield Farm's got a new owner – just like that."

Rachel Amsbary, the oldest of the three Amsbary daughters, had been listening to this exchange in silence. Her *mamm* was always well informed as to the goings-on in

Faith's Creek and had taken great delight in informing the family at dinner that night of the details of their new neighbors.

"When do they arrive?" her sister, Melinda, asked, and Victoria shrugged her shoulders as she cleared the plates from the table. "I'm not sure, exactly. This week, I think. We'll call on them when they arrive. Make sure they get a *gut* welcome."

Rachel caught her *daed's* eye and tried hard to suppress a smile. She knew exactly what her *mamm* intended by planning to call on their new neighbors. Her interest was not in a welcome or their background, where they came from, or what they intended to do now they had arrived in Faith's Creek – those were mere periphery details to discuss whilst gathering the actual information she required. Rachel's *mamm* was intent on seeing her daughters married, and if the new arrivals at Clearfield Farm came with sons, she would be only too happy.

"I'm sure they'll welcome a visit, you could take some of the apples we harvested last week," Abel said, smiling at Victoria.

"A family, Abel. That could mean sons." Victoria's smile was eager.

"Oh, *Mamm*, that's all you're interested in." Rachel rolled her eyes as she rose from the table.

There was not an evening went by in the Amsbary household where the subject of marriage was not raised. Sometimes it was subtle, sometimes it was blunt. Their *mamm* made no secret of the fact she wanted to see all three of her daughters happily married. She was forever seeking out possibilities, and there was not an eligible young man in Faith's Creek who had not found himself invited for a slice of shoofly pie in the parlor of the Amsbary farmhouse.

"I've got three girls, Rach – all of them at the age to wed. What else do you think I think of all day?"

Rachel smiled, glancing at her two sisters, who exchanged looks.

Rachel was the eldest at twenty-two, next came Melinda at twenty, and Sadie was the baby at only eighteen years old. She had just returned from her *rumspringa* in Philadelphia, and despite the high hopes that their *mamm* had attached to her departure from Faith's Creek, no prospective suitor had been forthcoming. The sisters were as alike as peas in a pod, each with the same blonde hair they had inherited from their *mamm*. Each was pretty in her own way, but strong-willed and independent, too – a trait they had inherited from their *daed*.

"There's no need to rush. Besides, these new folks – what's their name again? They might turn up with three daughters just like us," Abel said with a wink to the girls.

Victoria tutted and scowled at him. "The Sawyers, and don't talk like that, Abram. Don't you want your daughters to settle down and be happy?"

"Of course I do, but… I don't want my little lovelies marrying just anyone. We don't know anything about these Sawyers – they've got money, clearly, but… well, I only want what's best for these three," and he glanced at Rachel and smiled.

Abel had always referred to Rachel, Melinda, and Sadie as his "three lovelies." He doted on them, and whilst their *mamm* longed to see the three of them married and settled down, their *daed* would gladly have kept them in the family home for as long as possible. He was always suspicious of any man Victoria brought to the house, never believing anyone to be good enough for his daughters, each of whom he loved dearly.

"And that's why we'll call on them – to get to know them. I'm sure anyone coming from Ohio must be a decent sort," Victoria said.

Rachel could not help but laugh at her *mamm's* highfalutin tones.

"Why does that matter? Aren't there any *gut* men in Faith's Creek?" she asked, but Victoria was no longer listening and had retreated to the kitchen exclaiming something about only wanting the best for her daughters.

"Once she gets an idea into her head..." Abel said, shaking his head and rising from the table. "I love her but she has this need to see you all married. Me, I think that *Gott* will see to it in His time.

He pulled on his boots and stepped out onto the porch, leaving the three sisters alone at the table.

"I'd better go and help *mamm*," Sadie said, rising to her feet.

She took the empty dishes into the kitchen and Rachel glanced at Melinda, who smiled, each of them knowing what the other was thinking.

"Love or marriage, isn't that always the choice?" Melinda said, sighing as she sat back in her chair.

"I still think there's the hope of having both," Rachel replied.

She had been introduced to so many suitors but was yet to find a man she could truly fall in love with. Faith's Creek was full of eligible young men, all with admirable qualities, but Rachel was yet to find the one who could ignite a spark in her, one she could truly fall in love with.

"Oh, but it'll be just the same as it always is, Rach. You know how it is. *Mamm* gets excited about some new arrival, she parades us in front of them, and that's that."

Rachel smiled. She knew her sister was speaking the truth. The Sawyers would be no different from the Eckharts, or the Masts, or the Rabers, or any other family whom their *mamm* had believed represented the possibility of marital bliss for her three daughters.

"Just grin and bear it. That's all we can do," Rachel replied, just as their *mamm* appeared from the kitchen with her sleeves rolled up, her arms covered in soap suds.

"Are you two going to sit there all evening or are you going to come and help?"

Rachel and Melinda rose from the table, smiling at one another as they followed her into the kitchen where Sadie was busy drying plates and stacking them on the rack.

"When are we visiting the Sawyers, *Mamm*?" Melinda asked, picking up a dishcloth and beginning to dry the dishes which were stacked on the draining board next to the sink.

"We'll let them get settled in – a day or so afterward, perhaps. I don't want anyone else getting in there before us."

"You make it sound like there's a plot against us," Rachel said, causing their *mamm* to tut.

"You know what happened with Rachel Troyer and her daughters. Both married to the Coblentz boys, and why was that?" she asked.

"Because we didn't visit the day after meeting them at the market," the three sisters responded in chorus.

The incident with the Coblentz boys – two eligible young men from Philadelphia who had come to stay with an aunt in Faith's Creek and had married Luna and Alma Troyer some three weeks after their arrival – was a sore reminder for Victoria, one which was often raised in moments such as this.

"But there aren't any other women looking for husbands at the moment. Not in Faith's Creek, I mean," Sadie said, stacking the last of the plates into the rack.

"*Nee*, because they're all married. Three daughters, that's what I've got – three unmarried daughters. I don't know how I face the ladies at the quilting bees, I really don't. Sadie, you're only eighteen, there's time yet, but Rach and Mel… oh, I'm starting to despair. It's my prayer that *Gott* will send us three young men from Ohio, three Sawyer boys for my three girls," Victoria said, clapping her hands together in delight as though the prayer had already been answered.

There was little point in arguing, and Rachel finished her chores as quickly as possible, before making her way outside to take the evening air on the porch. It was late summer, and the evenings in Faith's Creek were still warm and balmy. She found her *daed* sitting out on the porch on the swing chair. He looked up at her and smiled, just as a shooting star traced its path through the night sky above.

"Is your *mamm* still preoccupied with our new neighbors?" he asked.

Rachel nodded, coming to sit down next to him on the swing chair. "She won't be happy until we're all wedded. It doesn't matter who to. She wants to see it happen."

"She means well, and I can see her point. She just wants you all to be happy, that's all."

Rachel knew he was right. She loved both her parents dearly, even if her *mamm* could be overbearing at times. But she did not want a mere marriage of arrangement. She wanted to fall in love, to be swept off her feet, to feel the way she knew so many other women had felt when those first tender feelings emerged.

"Well, maybe she'll get her wish," Rachel replied.

"I hope so, my love." He smiled and bid her goodnight.

Rachel sat alone in the darkness and prayed, could she have it all, or would she have to settle? Surely, there was more to life than just a marriage, just an arrangement?

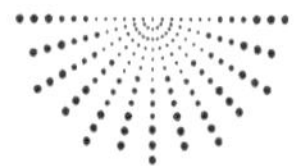

"Two sons, that's what Sarah Beiler told me. Two sons," Victoria exclaimed.

She had not even removed her shawl or set down her basket, desperate, it seemed, to share the news she had just learned.

Rachel had been making peanut butter cookies in the kitchen, but she had come through to the parlor where her two sisters were sitting by the stove, smiling as their *mamm* continued to extol the supposed virtues of their soon-to-be neighbors.

"But that doesn't bode well. Two sons and three of us. Who's going to miss out?" Melinda asked, glancing from Rachel to Sadie and back with a cheeky grin on her face.

"It's not a given that either of them would marry either of us. We might all miss out," Rachel replied, winking to her sisters when their *mamm* wasn't looking.

"Don't say such dreadful things, Rach. My nerves won't stand it. Besides, there's more," Victoria replied, and she took off her shawl and straightened her *kapp,* smiling at them and pausing for dramatic effect. "There's a cousin, too."

"A cousin? Is the whole family moving down?" Sadie asked.

"Three boys, count them, one, two, three, and three daughters, one, two, three," Victoria said, clapping her hands together.

Rachel shook her head and returned to the kitchen. The timer on the counter had just pinged. Grabbing some oven gloves, she took out the batch of cookies and slid them onto a cooling rack. They smelled sweet and buttery. She was making them for her friend, Tessa, and once they were cooled – and she had been forced to hear further details concerning the new arrivals from Ohio – Rachel set off to make the short walk across the fields to the house her friend shared with her new husband, Jacob Gascho, who, by coincidence, also hailed from Ohio.

* * *

"Oh, you didn't need to make cookies – though I won't say *nee* to one, or perhaps two. I'll make us some coffee to have with them. Sit down, won't you?" Tessa said, ushering Rachel into her parlor.

The two women had been friends ever since school, a friendship in which each of them was able to share anything that was troubling them. Tessa was a pretty young woman, with brown hair and deep blue eyes. She and Jacob had met on their *rumspringa*, and their relationship had blossomed in the coming years, leading to their marriage, which had taken place in Faith's Creek the previous summer.

"Did you hear about our new neighbors, the Sawyers? They've bought the whole of Clearfield Farm," Rachel said when Tessa had made the coffee and the two of them were sitting opposite one another by the parlor stove.

"Do they have sons?"

Rachel smiled. Tessa knew all about her *mamm's* intentions, and any newcomer to Faith's Creek was certain to be judged firstly on the number of eligible young men they arrived with.

"They do, two sons, and a cousin. You can imagine what it's like back home. *Mamm's* intent on visiting them as soon as possible. They'll still be unpacking the furniture when we come knocking," she replied.

"Is that the Sawyers?" Jacob asked.

He had been making himself a sandwich in the kitchen, but came through to the parlor and greeted Rachel warmly.

"I was going to ask if you knew them. Though Ohio's a big place," Rachel replied.

Jacob drew in a breath and the look on his face was troubling.

Rachel felt a tinge of worry, no matter what, her *mamm* would be determined to see them married, what if the family were awful?

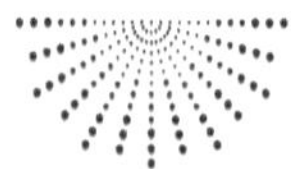

Jacob, a handsome man with dark hair and a long beard, sat down at the table and took a bite from his sandwich. He nodded, chewing ponderously before replying.

"I'm teasing," he said seeing the concern in Rachel's eyes.

She shook her head and let out a breath. "Oh, you."

Tessa punched his arm, playfully. "Now behave, and tell us about them."

Jacob laughed. "I've got ties to the family – we're somehow related, distant cousins, that sort of thing. But I've not seen them in years. Elmer and... Harley, that's right. They're the two sons. Good boys – well, men, now. I remember them when they were *kinner*. They're hard-working sorts. I'd let my daughter marry them," he said.

Rachel laughed. "I think it'll be a few years before you have to worry about that," she replied, laughing as Tessa blushed.

"Well... we're hoping to start a family soon, aren't we, Jacob?"

"I hope so," he said, taking another bite of his sandwich.

Rachel was thrilled at this news. She knew Tessa had always wanted a family, and that it would be a dream come true for her to have a *boppli* of her own.

"That's wonderful news. Still, it's a bit late for the Sawyer brothers. I think they might already be married by the time the *boppli* grows up, even if my *mamm* doesn't get her way."

"I'd like a boy, Tess wants a girl. We'll have to have one of each, I suppose," Jacob said.

"Or two of each..." Rachel said, and Tessa and Jacob laughed.

"Now, you're talking," Jacob said.

He took another bite of his sandwich, and Rachel offered him one of the cookies she had brought.

"They're delicious," Tessa said, helping herself to a third.

The talk returned to the new arrivals and Rachel was keen to know more about the Sawyer family, her curiosity aroused, even if she had no intention of marrying any of them.

"Do you know the cousin, too?" she asked.

To her surprise, Jacob's face turned grim, and he shook his head, pushing his plate aside with a sigh.

"I know *of* him, *jah*. He's bad news, though. David Knepp, that's his name. You don't want anything to do with him, believe me."

Rachel was surprised by his tone of voice. Jacob was always so mild-mannered and polite to a fault. She glanced at Tessa, who furrowed her brow, and set down her coffee cup.

"I hadn't made the connection – we met him once, didn't we? I took him to be a sweet tree with bad roots."

"Sweet tree? Rotten apple, more like. No, don't trust him, Rach. He's bad news, and your *mamm* won't be doing any of you three any favors if she presses a courtship with David," Jacob continued.

Rachel was intrigued. Far from being set against the possibility of meeting the wayward cousin, she found the thought of a man like that quite interesting. She was naturally attracted to rebellious types, especially considering she was often labeled as "headstrong." Jacob's description of David had roused her interest, and she was sensible enough to know that one man's bad apple could be another's sweet fruit.

"Might he just be a damaged soul?" she asked.

Jacob only shook his head. "I don't think so."

"I suppose we'll see if he's changed soon enough," Tessa said, rising to her feet to clear the empty coffee cups.

But when Rachel left the home of Tess and Jacob, her curiosity peaked. She wanted to know more about David Knepp, and to make up her own mind as to what he was like. When she arrived home, she found her sisters deep in conversation, and her *mamm* in a state of considerable excitement.

"They're here. They've arrived early. Your *daed* saw them on his way to market this morning in the buggy.

The parents, the two sons, and the cousin," Victoria said, clapping her hands together in delight.

"*Daed* says they're fine-looking men," Sadie said, as Rachel took off her shawl.

"Well, I know something, too," Rachel replied, and she proceeded to explain what she had learned from Jacob that morning.

But despite the excitement that these fresh details aroused, Rachel kept the opinion Jacob had of David Knepp a secret. She would make up her own mind as to what he was like, and she would not allow the opinions of others to influence her.

"They might attend the games night in Alf Bowman's barn," Melinda said after Rachel had finished describing the two brothers.

"That would be the perfect opportunity for the three of you to meet them – then we can call on them," Victoria said, a note of excitement entering her voice.

There was no doubt in Rachel's mind that change was coming, and that the possibility of romance was in the air. Her sisters and her *mamm* talked of nothing else, but Rachel's mind dwelled on the cousin, even as she wondered what he would be like.

"*A bad tree can still have good roots,*" she told herself, and, as the evening of the games night approached, Rachel found herself even more eager to meet the cousin who had so divided opinion in Ohio...

# CHAPTER FOUR

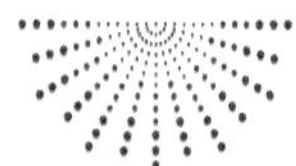

David Knepp surveyed the scene before him. The barn was busy, and the games night was in full swing. He and his sister had reluctantly come with his uncle and two cousins. He disliked such gatherings and the sort of people who attended them. He and his two cousins had been introduced to much of the community that evening – the Bishop, a man called Amos Beiler had done his best to make them feel welcome. But David felt out of place, and he was already thinking about his return to Ohio in a few weeks.

"What did you think of those three women?" his uncle, Iddo Sawyer asked.

David shrugged, even as his two cousins, Harley and Elmer, nodded enthusiastically.

"They were nice. I liked... Sadie, was it?" Elmer said, a broad smile spreading over his face.

Their first introduction had been to a family of three girls and their *mamm*. The Amsbarys had been presented by the Bishop's *fraa*, Sarah. David had endured the introductions through gritted teeth. There was no doubting the three women were pretty, but he knew precisely the reasons for their interest. David's uncle was a rich man, owing to the inheritance which he and David's *daed* had received, following the death of their dawdy some years ago. With David's *daed* having died a year or so ago, David had inherited his shared and was now a wealthy man in his own right, too.

"Sadie, and there was... Melinda and Rachel, the eldest," Harley said, grinning at his brother, even as David rolled his eyes.

"Is that all it takes? A pretty face and you're walking down the aisle?" he asked.

"Don't say that, David. Why can't Harley and Elmer dream a little? I'd like to see all three of you married – that's my only hope. I was just talking to their *mamm* – Victoria's her name – she's keen to make a more formal introduction," Iddo said.

David only gave an exasperated sigh. "Can't you see what they're doing, Uncle? It's always the same with these sorts of people. They're social climbers. They're on the lookout for men with money who can make their lives comfortable. What do the Englishchers call it? Gold diggers, that's right."

David had seen this type before. Women who did not give a second glance to a man until his wallet was opened and its contents revealed. They were fickle, and David prided himself on being able to see straight through them. His uncle looked at him in surprise, but David felt no shame in his harsh tone. The Amsbary women were just like all the rest, and he would not be turned by a pretty face and a flirtatious smile.

"I'm surprised at you, David," Iddo replied.

David shrugged his shoulders and reiterated his original point. "They're just looking to link themselves to better fortune, Uncle. If you can't see that, then... well, more fool you."

"It's not a nice way to be, David. You've got a terrible attitude toward people less fortunate than yourself. Don't forget, we came from nothing. Immigrants from Europe – your gross-dawdy..."

"Arrived with nothing from Europe and built an empire on a dollar. That's the American dream, Uncle. I know the story. It doesn't change the way other people think, though," David replied.

He had heard the same story told a hundred times, and he knew precisely what was coming next. His uncle drew himself up and fixed David with a stern expression.

"And I married a woman from a poor family, didn't I? Are you calling her a gold digger, too? I loved her, and she loved me – we built a happy home together and brought two fine sons into the world. What do you think of that?" Iddo said.

David rolled his eyes. It was always the same if he expressed an opinion about money. His uncle would leap to the defensive and remind him of the humble roots from which his aunt came, and of how she had loved him unconditionally – money had had no bearing on the matter.

"Well... I'm sure that's true, Uncle, but that doesn't mean all women are as good and honest as Aunt Liza," he replied.

His uncle scowled and turned away, leaving David and his two cousins alone.

"Why do you have to upset him like that, David?" Harley said.

David only waved his hand dismissively. "He knows what I think, and so do you. Couldn't you see what that silly woman was doing pushing her three daughters on us?"

"I liked her, I liked them, too," Elmer said, folding his arms.

David groaned. He knew he would not win the argument, even as he knew he was right, and he turned away, looking across the barn for his sister, Nancy, who had just risen from a game of trivia. She caught his eye and smiled, and he knew she knew just how much he was detesting the evening's activity.

"It'll be over soon," she whispered, coming to his side, and slipping her hand into his.

"It's all so predictable. Did you see that woman and her three daughters earlier on?"

"I saw you shaking hands, *jah*. Are you supposed to marry one of them?" she asked with a cheeky glint in her hazel eyes.

David smiled. He was glad of his sister's company. She understood him, and he understood her. Nancy was not taken in by foolish women and their daughters vying for the attentions of men with deep pockets.

"I think Harley and Elmer are swayed."

He glanced over to where his cousins were talking to two of the Amsbary girls, the youngest and the middle one. The eldest was sitting on her own drinking a glass of lemonade. She looked bored. David watched her for a moment, recalling the brief conversation they had shared.

*"You're Harley and Elmer's cousin. Yes, I heard about you,"* she had said, and David had found that a strange thing to say.

He wondered who it was who had told her something – anything – about him. As far as David knew, he knew no one in Faith's Creek, nor did he wish to.

"Let them be," his sister said. "They're the ones staying here. We're only here for a few weeks. Don't let the wayward charms of country girls get the better of you, David."

David nodded, but even as she spoke, he glanced again at the eldest of the three sisters. There was no doubting her obvious charms. She was pretty – beautiful, even – and he smiled at just how easily his two cousins had been swayed.

"*Not so for me,*" he told himself, glancing at the clock and hoping the evening's ordeal would soon be over.

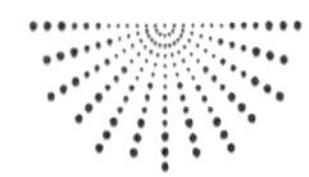

# CHAPTER FIVE

Rachel was bored. She had come to the games night caught up in the hopes of expectation foisted on her and her sisters by their *mamm*. But once the introductions had been made, she had found herself largely ignored. It had been Bishop Beiler who had brought the two families together. The Sawyers and the Amsbarys had been introduced, hands shaken, and pleasantries exchanged. Rachel had taken a liking to the affable Iddo Sawyer, and his two sons, Harley and Elmer, had soon paired off with Melinda and Sadie, leaving Rachel alone.

She had been uncertain what to expect from this first meeting with David, but apart from a brief exchange of pleasantries, little more had passed between them.

David had spent most of the evening talking to his sister, Nancy, and when she had availed herself of the game tables, he had stood alone in a corner, watching the proceedings with a scowl on his face. There was no doubting his attraction – his dark hair and hazel eyes were set in a handsome face, but his demeanor left much to be desired.

*"Perhaps Jacob was right,"* she told herself, glancing at David across the barn.

But something about him intrigued her, and she was keen to know more about him, even if he had made it clear he was unwilling to offer anything more than pass the time of day.

"I'm so pleased to see them together," Victoria said, startling her from her thoughts as she spoke.

"Oh... you mean Melinda and Sadie? They're only talking to them, *Mamm*. A woman can talk to a man without the sound of wedding bells peeling in the distance," Rachel replied.

Victoria only tutted. "Oh, why won't you let me have my fun, Rach? You barely spoke to that man."

"He barely spoke to me. I can't help it if he's rude," Rachel retorted.

She resented being blamed for a supposed lack of effort on her part. David had shown no sign of interest in her, and there had been plenty of opportunities for him to talk to her if he had chosen to do so.

"Be persistent, speak to him, strike up a conversation. Just don't stand there looking like a sour lemon." Victoria shook her head and her hands were itching to push Rachel in his direction, but she knew that was a step too far.

Rachel rolled her eyes. She was not standing there like anything. She wanted to go home, even as a part of her felt a pang of jealousy at the sight of her sisters having such success with the two Sawyer brothers. Her *mamm* wandered off to find her *daed*, and Rachel was once again left alone, glancing at David, who was now standing on his own in a far corner of the barn.

*"Just go and talk to him. What's to lose?"* she told herself, knowing she too deserved the happiness her sisters were enjoying at that very moment.

She took a deep breath and, even against her better judgment, crossed the barn to where David stood watching the proceedings with his arms folded.

"It gets a bit boring on your own, doesn't it?" she said, smiling at him and holding out her hand.

"We met earlier, didn't we?" he replied, shaking her hand.

Rachel nodded, glancing back at her two sisters. "I'm Rachel, Bishop Beiler introduced us. Aren't you going to play any games?"

"I don't care for games."

Rachel laughed. "It's a funny thing to come to a games night and not play games."

He shrugged and made no answer.

Rachel felt suddenly awkward. This was not going as she had anticipated. "How do you like Faith's Creek?" she asked, trying a different tack.

"I like it well enough – you're very forward, aren't you?" he said.

Rachel blushed. "I... well, the shy one gets nothing, I suppose," she replied, thinking she had offended him, but she was surprised to see a slight smile come over his face.

He nodded. "I like a person to be forward – we should say what we mean a lot more. Don't you think?"

Rachel nodded. She had always been one to speak her mind, even if it had gotten her into trouble at times. The slight smile on his face made him look different, and she could not help but warm to him ever so slightly, even as the questions as to Jacob's description of him as a rotten apple remained.

"I do, and I know you think I'm just looking for a husband," she replied.

Her words caused David to blush, and he shook his head, even as Rachel knew she had caught him out.

"Well, I..." he began, but she shook her head and laughed.

"It's all right – that's what my *mamm* intended. She wanted us to come here and find husbands. That's all we're good for in her eyes."

"And is that why you came over here?" he asked.

"I came over here because you looked bored out of your mind, and I wasn't faring much better. Why don't we take a walk outside? It's getting awfully hot and stuffy in here," she said, and, in a surprising gesture, he offered her his arm, the two of them stepping through the throng of gamers and out of the double doors into the cool of the farmyard.

It was a cool night, and the moon was full, the stars twinkling in the sky above. They walked as far as the farm gate, pausing to lean on it, the sounds of the games night in the barn drifting through the still night air.

"It's a nice enough place, I suppose," David said, as they gazed out over the horizon.

"What's Ohio like?" Rachel asked.

Despite being twenty-two years old, she had barely left Faith's Creek and had not joined Tessa and the others on their *rumspringa*. She often wondered what life was like in other places and for other people. She was curious about the world and liked to learn more about it whenever she could.

"It's nice enough. My uncle's just swapped one big farm for another. I don't know why he wanted to come down here. I don't think I'll be staying long."

"You're not sticking around?" she asked.

He shook his head. "My sister and I have our *daed's* property to deal with back home. There's a lot to think about."

There was an arrogant tone in his voice, as though he was trying to make out his own self-importance. Rachel was not impressed by wealth in any form. She was not interested in money or the prestige it could bring. Her needs and tastes were simple, and she was happy without the trappings of wealth.

"Are you selling it?" she asked, curious, still, to know more about his past.

But his reaction to her innocent question came as quite a surprise. She felt him stiffen at her side and he turned to her with an angry expression on his face.

"What business is it of yours if we're selling it? You're all the same, aren't you?" he exclaimed.

Rachel stared at him in amazement. "I was only asking to make conversation. I'm curious but nothing more," she retorted, for she was not about to be spoken to in such a way by a man she barely knew.

"Curious about the money, I suppose. It's always the same. Well, what do you know about dealing with a plot of land, selling it, or otherwise?"

Rachel was growing angry now. He had no right to speak to her in such a way and she fixed him with a hard stare, determined not to let him get away with such an appalling attitude.

"Is that how you always speak to women? As if they're nothing but a nuisance for daring to ask an innocent question? I don't care one bit about your property. Sell it, keep it. What do I care?"

David looked somewhat taken aback by her response. It was clear he had little experience of speaking to women, and that his attitude towards Rachel was preconceived. It had been a mistake on her part to think he would behave any differently from the cold shoulder of their first introduction. Rachel had heard enough, and she stepped back, still holding his gaze defiantly.

"I don't have to explain myself to you," he retorted.

Rachel gave an exasperated cry. "Well, then, it seems your reputation preceded you, didn't it?"

David looked at her in surprise, but she gave him no time to reply, turning on her heels and marching back across the farmyard, her clenched fists shaking with anger. He had assumed her interest lay purely in his financial situation, that she was merely interested in what benefit she could derive from association with him. Rachel could not have cared less whether he was rich or poor, but of one thing, she was now certain: money was no precursor to manners.

"I saw you step out with the cousin. Did you make a good impression?" her *mamm* asked, as Rachel returned to the barn.

Rachel gave her a cold look, folding her arms as she spoke.

"I wasn't the one who needed to make it," she retorted.

Victoria looked at her in surprise. "Oh, Rach, don't spoil this for your sisters. Look at them, they're getting on very well indeed," she said, pointing across the barn to where Melinda and Sadie were standing talking to the two brothers.

Rachel rolled her eyes. She had no intention of spoiling her sisters' happiness, but neither did she intend to spoil her own either. She had tried to be friendly towards David, her curiosity leading her to ask him questions that he had mistaken for prying rather than genuine interest. But he had been so rude to her that Rachel had no intention of ever speaking to him again – whether it caused her *mamm* distress or not.

"I won't spoil it for anyone, but I'm telling you this, I don't want anything to do with David Knepp. I should've listened to Jordan instead of letting my curiosity get the better of me," and without waiting for her *mamm* to reply, Rachel snatched up her shawl and left the barn, vowing to have nothing to do with the Sawyers again...

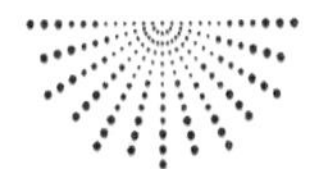

# CHAPTER SIX

"I'm off to the creek with Elmer," Sadie called out, appearing from the kitchen with a picnic basket tucked under her arm.

She was dressed in summer clothes with a large straw hat on her head and a smile on her face.

"I hope you've got your *kapp* on under that," Rachel said, raising her eyebrows, even as their *mamm* clapped her hands together in excitement.

"She will have. Oh, you'll have a wonderful time, Sadie. Enjoy yourself. Did you remember to pack the cinnamon swirls I made yesterday?"

"And the cornbread salad," Sadie replied.

She ignored Rachel's question and hurried out of the door onto the porch, her footsteps clattering across the yard, just as Melinda's voice came from upstairs.

"Has anyone seen my outdoor shoes? I can't find them anywhere."

"Have you tried the rack on the porch?" Victoria called back, and a moment later, Melinda appeared on the stairs, a smile spread over her face.

"I'd forget my head if it wasn't screwed on. I'm all at sixes and sevens today. Isn't it exciting?"

Melinda had been invited to help Harley in the garden at Clearfield Farm. The Sawyers were planting up the vegetable plots and cutting back the overgrowth in the orchards to reveal the fruit trees, which had long since been lost in the encroachment of nature.

They rarely wore shoes so it was obvious that her sister was trying to impress.

"You're only going to do some weeding," Rachel said.

Melinda shook her head. "But *he's* invited me to help," she replied, as though that fact made all the difference.

"Have a wonderful time, Mel," Victoria said, beaming at Melinda, who was now putting on her shawl. "Oh... to think, one daughter out on a picnic, the other away to the farm, both with their handsome young men in tow," and a few moments later, Melinda had hurried out of the house, calling out her goodbyes.

Rachel rolled her eyes. It seemed everyone was caught up in the romance of the handsome brothers and whilst she was happy for her sisters, Rachel could not help but feel a slight sadness that things had not worked out quite so well for her, even as she reminded herself that the third of the Sawyer boys was far from a suitable match.

"Are you sure about letting Sadie go off to the creek like that for a picnic?" Rachel asked, but her *mamm* only waved her hand dismissively and nodded.

"Why wouldn't I be? I want my daughters to be happy. If it was up to your *daed*, you'd all be wrapped in cotton wool and never allowed to leave the house. You can't live your lives like that, but... oh, it's such a shame."

Rachel looked at her curiously, wondering what she meant.

"A shame?" she asked.

Victoria sighed. "That you and the cousin didn't find some common ground together. I don't know what went on between you, but... isn't there still a chance for the two of you?"

Rachel shook her head. The more she thought about David, the angrier she became. He had made a judgment on her, a presumption that her only interest lay in the sale of his *daed's* property, a sale which would make an already wealthy man even wealthier. The truth was very different, but Rachel had no intention of trying to explain herself. She wished she had listened to Jordan and avoided David entirely. He was a rude, arrogant man, and Faith's Creek would be no poorer when he and his sister returned to Ohio.

"There's *nee* chance, *nee*. I don't want anything to do with him," she replied.

Victoria shook her head. "Well... if you're sure. I know I come across as a silly old woman sometimes, but I really do just want all three of you to be happy. That's my only hope."

Rachel smiled, reaching out to take her *mamm's* hand in hers.

"I know you do, *Mamm*. But I... I didn't like him. I tried to be friendly, and he just threw it back in my face. What can I do about that? There're other men in Faith's

Creek. I don't have to put all my eggs in one basket, do I? If you get two daughters married to the Sawyers, that's *gut* enough, isn't it?"

Victoria squeezed her hand, a sad look coming over her face, and Rachel knew that it was her, and not the others, whom she worried about the most. Sadie was only eighteen and barely at the beginning of her search for a husband, and Melinda, though two years older, still had plenty of time. But Rachel was, to use the unfortunate term which others had already applied, approaching the status of an "old maid." It was not that she was unhappy with her lot – far from it – but a part of her longed to marry, though she would not settle for anything other than true love.

"I know you tried, but... wouldn't you want to try again? Perhaps he was just having a bad night or had something on his mind. We can all be rude at times." Victoria shrugged and smiled hopefully, but Rachel was not interested in hearing anything more.

They could discuss the apparent merits of David Knepp until they were blue in the face, but it would not change her mind about him. First impressions were important, and David's first impression had left nothing but a sour taste in her mouth.

"There's nothing you can say that'll change my mind. I don't want anything to do with him anymore. I'd rather be an old maid than marry a man like him," she exclaimed, banging her fist down on the arm of the chair she was sitting in, just as her *daed* came in from the porch.

"Are we still talking about this?" he asked, raising his eyebrows.

Since the games night, the talk in the Amsbary household had revolved around little else but the arrival of the Sawyers and Rachel knew her *daed* was growing tired of the constant references to marriage and courtship. She glanced at him and smiled, knowing he would take her side against her *mamm's* insistence on giving David another chance.

"I'm only trying to talk some sense into Rachel. She won't listen. She's as stubborn as you, Abel. I know where she gets it from." Victoria shook her head and tutted. "All I want is for our daughters to be happy. Look at Melinda and Sadie. They've gone off happily today to meet those two young men – and what charming young men they are. I don't see why..."

"You don't see why our eldest has to speak her own mind on the matter?" Abel cut her off mid-flow.

"Exactly, she's..." Victoria began, but Abel only laughed and shook his head.

"Because it's her own mind to make up. If she's made her choice, then we've got to respect that, Victoria, and not expect her to follow what we might think is for the best. Besides, we don't know anything about those two brothers. They might prove a different type altogether, we just don't know. But let the girls make their own mistakes and their own decisions."

Victoria narrowed her eyes. She looked disgruntled, but she made no further attempts at persuasion, even as Rachel smiled at her *daed* and mouthed a silent thank you. She knew her *mamm* only meant well, and that in her eyes, happiness was only to be found in the manner she herself had found it: by marrying a man and settling down into a life of domesticated certainty. But such an outcome was in no way guaranteed, and Rachel knew that unless she married a man she had truly fallen in love with, happiness would elude her.

She thought of Tessa and Jacob, perfectly matched and the happiest of couples. That was what she desired, and she was under no illusion that David Knepp would be the one to fulfill that desire – even if he wanted to, and that she sincerely doubted.

"Well, we'll just have to see what comes of it," Victoria said having the last word before rising to her feet and making her way into the kitchen, where she could soon be heard loudly banging pots and pans.

"You know I'll always support you, Rach," Abel said.

Rachel smiled as he put his arms around her and kissed her on the forehead. "I know you will, *Daed*, even if I make a few mistakes along the way."

But Rachel was determined not to allow David Knepp to be one of those mistakes, and in the coming days, she tried her best to put him out of her mind.

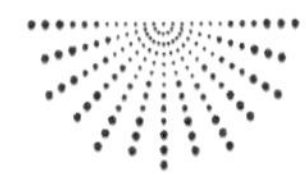

# CHAPTER SEVEN

David was watching his cousin, Harley with amusement. He was balanced precariously on a long ladder leaned into an ancient apple tree in the orchard. At the base of it, Melinda Amsbary was standing, looking fearfully up as Harley reached out to clip the boughs of the tree with a large pair of shears.

"Oh, Harley, be careful up there," she exclaimed as Harley almost fell into the foliage, and several unripened apples fell to the ground with a series of thuds.

"I'll be all right, Mel. Just hold the ladder tightly," Harley called back.

David shook his head and rolled his eyes. He had been watching this bizarre example of courtship from the porch for the past half an hour. Melinda had come to the farm almost every day since the games night, and if she was not there, then Harley was likely to be across the fields, sitting on the porch of the Amsbary farmhouse. The two were courting, and it seemed they were inseparable. The same could be said for Elmer and Sadie, and the two of them were forever off picnicking by the creek or taking walks on the ridge.

David could only remain skeptical as to the two sister's intentions, but despite his warnings to Harley and Elmer, it seemed his two cousins were besotted. He smiled to himself, feeling smug that he had seen through the Amsbary sister's intentions. They were gold diggers. It was as simple as that, and David had made his views clear to both his uncle and his two cousins – none of whom had paid the slightest attention to him.

"You're just jealous because Rachel Amsbary turned you down," Elmer had retorted, words which had caused David to scoff.

"Nonsense. I turned her down. I don't need a gold digger coming after me. If you can't see what's right in front of you, then more fool you," David had replied, and that was how the matter had been left.

But try as he might, David had been unable to rid himself of the thought that perhaps Rachel was different. It was his sister who had planted a further seed against the oldest of the three sisters, reminding David that their *mamm* was an opportunist and would do anything she could to push forward her own agenda.

"Don't go soft on the idea, David. They're all the same," she had told him, even as David had wondered if the opposite were true.

He had heard nothing from Rachel in the days following the games night, not that he wished to, but it had surprised him she had made no further attempts to entice him. She wanted money out of him, of that, he was certain, and it had seemed odd that she had made no move to ingratiate herself to his favor.

*"She walked away from you,"* he told himself, as he sat on the swing chair on the porch watching his cousin and Melinda in the orchard.

He had expected her to try something else to win him around, some other ploy to make him malleable to her charms. But silence had been her response, and David was not used to silence. He had encountered many women before whose sole object was the wealth that was his. They had not been interested in him, but rather in what he could give them. It had pained him, even as he had made sure to guard himself against such greed on the part of others.

"Look at them, he hasn't got a clue, has he?" Nancy said, appearing on the porch with a cup of coffee in her hand.

"He's fallen for her, all right," David replied, as his sister sat down next to him, the aroma of coffee filling the air with its aromatic scent.

"She's manipulating him, just like the other one tried to manipulate you. They must all have a good laugh back home every night – laughing at Harley and Elmer for being so naïve."

"Do you think so? It looks pretty genuine to me," David said, even as a part of him did not wish to believe his own words.

He did not like to admit it but he felt a certain level of jealousy toward his two cousins. He had never seen them happier than they had been in the past few days, and it seemed that arriving in Faith's Creek had brought with it a new lease of life for them both. Whilst David would often behave as though he were on the defensive, his feelings were far more complex. He liked the idea of meeting someone and settling down, even if, so far, he had found it hard to do so.

"It's not genuine. Don't go soft on me now," Nancy said. "Can't you see what she's doing? Her and her sister. I'm surprised the eldest one hasn't been sniffing around again. You'd think their *mamm* would want to make it a full house." Nancy curled her lip and shook her head.

"She was the one who turned away from me. I was... surprised by what she said."

Nancy uttered an exclamation of doubt and rose to her feet, tutting at him as she did so.

"Oh, nonsense. I knew this would happen. You've been taken in by the charms of a country girl. The sooner we get back to Ohio, the better." With this, she stormed off back inside, banging the porch door behind her.

David had been quick to agree with his sister as to Rachel's motives. But the more he had thought about it, the more uncertain he had become as to the truth of his own thoughts. The fact that she turned away from him – was rude even – suggested something about her character, something which had nothing to do with money. In the past, when David had sought to get rid of gold diggers, he had found them nothing but persistent. He had expected Rachel to be the same, but he had heard nothing from her, and it seemed she had simply cut him off.

*"I suppose Nancy would say it was all a ploy,"* he thought to himself, rising from the swing and making his way down the porch steps and across to the orchard.

Harley was still balanced precariously on the top of the ladder, and a sudden shower of apples caused Melinda to let go of the base. The ladder wobbled, and she gave a cry as Harley lurched forward and fell into the branches of the tree.

"Oh, my goodness, help!" Melinda exclaimed.

David leaped over the fence, just in time to see his cousin swinging from one of the branches, laughing, as he dropped to the ground.

His dungarees were all torn, and his face was scratched, but he caught his breath, still laughing as Melinda ran to throw her arms around him.

"I'm all right. The branches broke the fall. But when I say hold on, I mean it," he said.

"I'm so sorry. Look at you, you're all scratched. Let's get you back to the house," she said, glancing at David.

"You've got to marry him before you get his money," David said shaking his head.

Harley looked up at him and scowled. "Don't say that, David. It makes you look like an idiot."

Melinda swallowed, her eyes filled with hurt as she took Harley by the arm, and they made their way out of the orchard gate and across the farmyard.

David shook his head, even as he knew the tone of Melinda's voice had been sincere. She had been genuinely fearful, and he wondered if perhaps his words had been somewhat harsh. He stooped down and picked up one of the apples, taking a bite out of it and grimacing. The fruit was sour, yet to ripen in the summer sun, and he tossed it aside, the bitter taste remaining in his mouth as he walked across the farmyard after Harley and Melinda.

*"Maybe I've misjudged them all,"* he said to himself, even if he would not dare to admit as much to Nancy...

# CHAPTER EIGHT

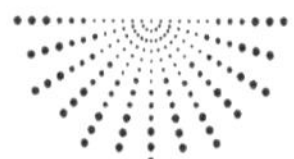

Melinda had never felt so happy as she did now. There was no doubt that Harley had fallen in love with her, and she had fallen in love with him. She had never experienced such feelings before, and to be swept off her feet in such a manner was a delight beyond words.

She had been terrified at the sight of him falling through the branches of the apple tree, but the relief in her heart at his being all right had only served to confirm the feelings she had for him. She had insisted on remaining at the Sawyer farmhouse that afternoon and had prepared a chicken soup for Harley, knowing it was the sort of thing a person did when someone was sick.

"You really don't have to, Mel," Harley had said, but Melinda had insisted.

The two of them had sat together for the afternoon by the stove as Melinda prepared the chicken soup and they talked constantly about life in Faith's Creek.

"You'll stay here, won't you? You don't want to go back to Ohio?" she asked, placing a tray with a bowl of soup and a hunk of cornbread on it in front of him.

"Go back to Ohio? When I've met a woman like you? I don't think so." He smiled at her, taking up his spoon as Melinda blushed.

At that moment, the door opened, and David appeared. He pulled off his boots and tossed them to one side, glancing at Melinda and Harley with a nod.

Melinda had not warmed to David. She found him rude and bordering on arrogant. The way he had spoken to her had been nothing short of accusatory. Harley had explained that David and his sister believed the Amsbary sisters were only interested in the Sawyer brother' money.

"How's the patient?" David asked.

"I'm fine, I don't need all this fuss, even if it's nice," Harley replied, glancing at Melinda, and smiling.

"Well… it's very kind of you to stick around," David said, fixing Melinda with a curious expression as she narrowed her eyes, confused by David's sudden change in attitude towards her.

She could not tell if he was sincere or not. "Why wouldn't I stay? Harley's had a nasty shock, and my *mamm* always says the best cure for a shock is a bowl of chicken soup."

"Well, we've got plenty of chickens, I suppose," David replied, and without waiting for an answer, he made his way upstairs.

Melinda glanced at Harley, and the two of them shrugged, each suppressing their laughter, which burst forth as soon as they heard David's bedroom door close above.

"You and your cousin are so different. You'd never guess you were related," Melinda said, shaking her head as she continued to eat from her bowl of soup.

"He's harmless enough, but… he can be… uncharitable, that's for sure," Harley replied.

Melinda did not like to think badly of anyone, but she had heard her *mamm* and Rachel talking about an encounter between her sister and David at the games night. She had not liked to ask too many questions, even as she had known how upset her *mamm* had been that all three of her daughters had not found the expected romance. But Melinda was happy – she had found a man to fall in love with, and it seemed he had fallen in love with her. She would happily have spent all her days at Clearfield Farm, happy in Harley's company, and at last realizing what true love could mean. She had had other suitors, but none like Harley, whose kind words and handsome features had entirely swept her off her feet.

"I'm sure he could change. Anyone can change if they're given a chance to," she said.

Harley shrugged. "Well... perhaps, but... let's not think about David." He smiled at her, complimenting her again on the excellent soup which really had made him feel better.

When Melinda returned home later that afternoon, she found her *mamm* in a state of great excitement. Sadie had just returned from a picnic with Elmer and was full of the joys of being in love. Melinda felt it, too, and she shared with her *mamm* and sister the drama of the ladder in the orchard, and how she had helped Harley in the aftermath of his fall.

"That's perfect, Mel. He'll remember that. Oh... my two daughters falling in love, what more could a *mamm* want?"

Even as she spoke, Melinda noticed a look of sadness in her eyes, and she knew her *mamm* was thinking of Rachel. There was one more thing to want, and that was happiness for the eldest of the three. Melinda felt sorry for Rachel and guilty for finding happiness when her sister was deprived of it.

"You should've heard the way Elmer spoke to me today. He told me I was beautiful, and that he'd happily spend every waking moment with me," Sadie said, swooning as she sat back on a chair by the stove and breathed a deep sigh of satisfaction.

"It's the same with Harley," Melinda said.

Victoria – having recovered from her moment of sadness – clapped her hands together in delight. "We'll have proposals soon."

Melinda glanced at Sadie with a smile. There was no doubt in her mind that if Harley proposed, her answer would be yes, and she was certain her sister would say the same to Elmer. The thought made her feel happier than she could express, and her mind wandered to marriage vows and domesticity. It was what she had been raised to want – just as her *mamm* wanted it, too – and the thought of being so close to such happiness was quite overwhelming.

"I'm going to go up to the farm again tomorrow. We're going to sow beets in the garden," Melinda said, just as Rachel appeared on the stairs.

Melinda was unsure of how to greet her sister. Rachel had seemed ponderous in the past few days, and it seemed she was carrying a burden, one which Melinda felt sad to see. She thought of David and his odd behavior up at the farm that afternoon...

"Did you have a nice time today?" Rachel asked, glancing from Melinda to Sadie and back.

"I had a wonderful time, Elmer's so sweet. He took me on the most delightful picnic down by the creek. We're going for a walk on the ridge tomorrow," Sadie said, oblivious, it seemed, to any feelings which Rachel might have to the contrary.

But Melinda could hardly blame Sadie for being so caught up in the happiness she had found. It was a happiness she, too, shared, and it saddened her to think that Rachel could not share in it with them.

"I'm sure it's all very nice," Rachel replied, sitting down in a chair next to the stove.

Melinda rose to make coffee for them, and as she did so, she slipped her hand into her pocket, surprised to find a piece of folded paper there.

*"What's this?"* she said to herself, drawing out the piece of paper and unfolding it.

It was a note, signed from Harley – he must have slipped it into her pocket when she was making the chicken soup – and in it, he spoke of how much the past few days had meant to him. He had never felt like this about anyone before – or so he said – and he wrote of how he wanted to spend every waking moment with her.

"What's that, Melinda?" Victoria asked.

Melinda looked up with a smile on her face. "It's a note from Harley. I didn't know it was there. He wants to *'meet me under a starlit sky'*. It's so romantic."

She handed the note to her *mamm*, blushing at the thought of Harley's attention. These feelings were new and exciting, and they filled her with hope for the future.

"Oh, isn't that lovely, and he says he wants to meet you again as soon as he can," Victoria said, but Melinda noticed Rachel roll her eyes.

"Is something wrong?" she asked

Rachel shook her head. "I'm... I'm just not sure about trusting a Sawyer."

Melinda looked at her in surprise. She had not spoken of such prejudice before, and Melinda could think of no reason not to trust Harley – or Elmer, or their *daed*. She narrowed her eyes, wondering if this was more about Rachel than about Harley.

"Why not?"

"I just... I don't want you to get hurt, either of you. You're both young and..." Rachel began, but Sadie interrupted her.

"You're just jealous. Listen to her, *Mamm*. She's just jealous of us both. There's not a bad word to be said about Elmer – or Harley. She's just bitter because David's not like his cousins. Elmer told me all about

David. He's the one you can't trust. Can't you just be happy for us?"

Victoria expressed similar sentiments, and whilst Melinda could feel sorry for her sister, she was not about to push Harley aside based on mere intuition. She kept thinking about the note, and of Harley's invitation to meet her "under a starlit sky". She knew where that would be – he had spoken about it that very morning. He had told her that from the orchard at Clearfield Farm, on a clear night, the skies opened up in a spectacular display of stars. He had camped out there frequently since arriving in Faith's Creek, lying on his back and gazing up into the skies above. It sounded ever so romantic, and Melinda's heart was beating fast at the thought of joining him.

"I'm happy for you, but I want you to make the right decision. You don't know them, not properly," Rachel replied.

"But that's the point of a courtship – to get to know them. Just be happy for your sisters, Rachel." Victoria gave her eldest daughter a sad look.

Rachel sighed, glancing at Melinda with a sorrowful expression on her face.

"Don't project your own doubts on us, Rachel. We're old enough to look after ourselves," Melinda said, folding up the note and replacing it in her pocket.

Her words sounded harsher than she meant them, but she was not about to allow her happiness – or that of Sadie's – to be overshadowed. She had no reason not to trust Harley, and their *mamm* was right – the point of courtship was to get to know someone and then make an informed decision. Melinda considered herself a good judge of character, and she was certain she had judged Harley correctly.

"I just hope you both know what you're doing," Rachel said, and without waiting for a reply, she hurried off into the kitchen.

"Don't listen to her, girls. You've each made the right choice. I know it," Victoria said.

Melinda smiled at her, anxious to see Harley again, and certain she had found the happiness which was destined to be hers. Rachel was just being silly, and yet her sister's doubts left an uneasy feeling in her stomach.

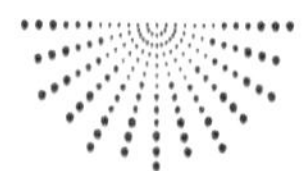

# CHAPTER NINE

Rachel sighed. She had done what she thought was best in raising doubts over Harley and Elmer. But her two sisters were so caught up in the flush of young love that they were deaf to any potential danger.

It was not that she had any specific reason to doubt the sincerity of the Sawyer brothers. They were charming, affable, likable, handsome – possessed of every possible quality which made them an attractive proposition. But Rachel knew that the apple never fell far from the tree and that one rotten piece of fruit could easily infect the rest. They knew nothing of the Sawyers, save from the fact of their wealth, and given her experience with David, Rachel had come to wonder if his cousins were truly the men they appeared to be.

*"Or is Sadie right? Am I just jealous?"* she asked herself.

It was a searching question, one which she found uncomfortable to contemplate. She did not like to think of herself as being jealous. Jealousy, as Bishop Beiler so often reminded the congregation, was an infection, one which could so easily eat up a person's soul. There were few things worse than being jealous, for jealousy was all-consuming and could leave a bitterness that was hard to shake. Rachel did not like to think of herself as being jealous, even though she realized she might be.

"Look, Mel, I'm sorry about earlier on," Rachel said when she met her sister on the landing at bedtime later that evening.

"I know you're only trying to protect me, Rach. It's sweet, but I don't need you to, all right?"

Rachel nodded. She knew her sister was grown up now. As *kinner*, Rachel had always been the one to take care of her two siblings. Seeing them turn into young women had been both a delight and a sorrow. She longed for the simple days when the three of them would play together by the creek or walk for miles along the ridge. They were happy days when the thought of marriage and men was but a distant dream.

However, Melinda and Sadie were no longer *kinner*. They were their own women, and Rachel felt tears well up in her eyes at the thought that she was no longer needed in the same way as before.

"I know..." Rachel replied, and she bid her sister goodnight.

But lying in bed that night, tossing and turning and trying to sleep, Rachel could not help but feel a sense of impending danger. There was something about the Sawyer brothers – about the family – that bothered her. Seeing her sisters so caught up in the romance of their situation worried her. It was late into the night before she slept, and she awoke to the sound of a cockerel crowing on Clearfield Farm. She sat up, her mind racing with the same thoughts she had fallen asleep with.

*"I need to speak to her,"* she told herself, and she rose from her bed and stepped out onto the landing.

She could hear her *daed* snoring in the bedroom at the far end of the landing, Sadie's door was firmly closed. But, to her surprise, Melinda's door was open, and pushing it wide, she found the bed empty – unslept in.

Her eyes grew wide with astonishment, and panic rose inside her. Melinda was gone!

Rachel remembered the note and Harley's words about a "starlit sky".

"Oh, Melinda, you fool," she exclaimed, and hurrying back to her bedroom she hastily dressed, putting on her *kapp* and shawl before hurrying downstairs and out onto the porch.

The sun was just rising on the horizon, casting its rays across the yard. With fear in her heart, Rachel set off in the direction of Clearfield Farm, determined to find her sister and bring her to her senses...

# CHAPTER TEN

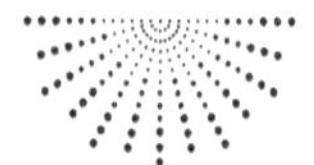

The way to Clearfield Farm passed between the cornfields, the crop catching the early morning sun appeared as a shimmering sea of gold. But Rachel hardly noticed it, her thoughts were elsewhere, and she could think only of finding her sister and saving her from any potential scandal.

It was clear to Rachel that Melinda was besotted with Harley, and when a woman was so caught up in her passions, there could be no telling what danger she could be in.

The thought of scandal was racing through Rachel's mind, but as she came to the crossroads which led either to the farm or into the center of the community, she paused. Footsteps were coming around the corner, hastening fast, but the view was obscured by the tall sheaves of corn.

Rachel paused, her heart in her throat, as she stared in surprise as none other than David Knepp appeared before her.

He seemed just as surprised to see her, too, and for a moment, they stood in silence, each blocking the other's path.

"You're in quite a hurry," she said.

He nodded, narrowing his eyes as it seemed he realized she was heading in the direction of Clearfield Farm.

"And so are you."

"I'm looking for my sister... have you seen her? Melinda, I mean. I think she's with your cousin."

"And why would I know anything about what my cousin was doing?" he asked.

Rachel shrugged her shoulders. He was being deliberately difficult, so she stepped to one side, eager to be on her way, knowing time was of the essence.

"Would you excuse me? You've got business, I've got business, and... where are you going?" she asked, no longer concerned at maintaining a polite disposition towards a man who had been so callous towards her.

"That's none of your business, but if you must know... I want to talk to Jacob Gascho," he replied.

At these words, Rachel's eyes grew wide with astonishment. She knew Jacob and David had had dealings in the past. It was Jacob who had warned her against trusting David in the first place. She remembered his words about rotten fruit, her eyes narrowing as she shook her head.

"They're my friends. What do you want with them?"

She spoke in a demanding tone. Tessa was in a delicate condition, they were trying for a baby, and Rachel was not about to allow David to upset her.

"I know what Jacob's been saying about me. He's put all sorts of rumors out about me. It won't do. He's too angry for his own *gut*. I know Jacob, and I know what he's really like."

Rachel was about to respond with an angry comeback. Tessa had been her friend since they were young, and Jacob had been nothing but a good husband to her. But she was stopped by the thought that perhaps – just perhaps – David was telling the truth. She had taken

Jacob's words at face value and had believed everything he had told her about the man standing before her. But he had given no reason for his explanation, no reason why David was all the things he had claimed him to be. Rachel stared at David, shaking her head, unsure of what to believe.

"I... you don't... I don't..." she began, feeling thoroughly confused.

"I just want to talk to him. I don't like it that such ugly things are being said about me," David said, his tone softening, even as his stance remained defiant.

"He told me about you... and I believed him," Rachel admitted.

She felt foolish to have done so, rather than make up her own mind on the matter. But the facts were as they were, and Rachel had judged David on the words of another, taking them at face value because Jacob was Tessa's husband.

"Well, maybe you shouldn't have."

Rachel felt a sudden sense of guilt. She hadn't intended to do so but with his behavior, she had judged David, and she knew well enough the teachings on judgment. To judge another was to behave as though you were

*Gott*, and terrible things would come of that. She could imagine Bishop Beiler raising his finger and warning the congregation about judgment.

"Judge not, else you'll be judged," he would say, and Rachel would feel her stomach twist in knots.

"No... perhaps not," she replied.

"We got off to a bad start, didn't we?" David said.

Rachel raised an eyebrow. "You could say that."

She thought back to the conversation outside the barn, how he had assumed her to be a gold digger and she, in turn, had offered little by way of rebuttal, storming off, instead of confronting him with the truth and trying to learn the truth about him. They were both to blame for preconceived ideas, and Rachel sighed, suddenly feeling terribly foolish.

"Then why don't we start again? Perhaps you've misjudged me... I know I've misjudged you," he said.

Rachel's heart was racing and, to her surprise, he reached out and took her by the hand, a smile coming over his face. Her doubts were fading, and she was willing to give him another chance, even if the risk seemed just the same as that which she had warned her sisters of only the evening before. Emotions did funny things to the reason, and Rachel swallowed hard, her hands trembling, even as he took a step forward.

"I think I might have done," she admitted, blushing, as he smiled at her.

"We all judge others prematurely. But... you can't truly judge a person until you know them."

Rachel nodded. She knew his words were true, and that she had done just that, even as he had surely done so, too. She smiled at him and was about to reply when a shout came from the lane leading towards Faith's Creek and Rachel turned to find Jacob hurrying towards them.

"Rach! Rach! Oh, thank goodness I've found you. I need help. It's Tessa. She's gone into labor."

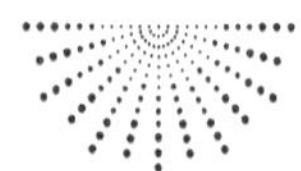

# CHAPTER ELEVEN

Rachel pulled her hand from David's and turned to Jacob in amazement. Tessa was not even pregnant. She knew the two of them were planning to start a family, but Tessa had only mentioned it to her a few days ago and she had shown no signs of pregnancy.

Jacob was breathless, a desperate look on his face, and he beckoned her to follow him, glancing at David as he did so.

"She can't be in labor, Jacob. She's not pregnant," Rachel exclaimed

Jacob responded angrily. "Don't you think I know that? But she is, I'm telling you. We didn't know, but... it can happen, can't it?"

"I... I don't know," Rachel stammered.

It was David who stepped up to the mark. "We need to get back to her. If she's in labor, then she needs help, and even if she isn't, it sounds like she's in terrible pain. Come on, it's this way, isn't it?" he asked.

Jacob glanced at Rachel, and it seemed he was about to object, but Rachel knew there was no time to lose, and she seized him by the hand, trying her best to reassure him.

"It's all right. We'll help her. She'll be fine, but we've got to get to her."

They hurried off along the lane towards the house, the three of them running together so that they were soon on the porch. Rachel could hear Tessa's cries from inside, and as they opened the door, they found her lying on the rug in front of the stove, clutching in agony at her stomach.

"Tess, I've got Rachel here. She'll help you," Jacob said, kneeling at his *fraa's* side.

Rachel glanced at David with a worried expression. She knew nothing about pregnancy, and certainly nothing about how to deliver a baby. Her hands were trembling, and she felt powerless to know what to do.

David once again stepped forward. His demeanor was calm and collected, and he kneeled next to Tessa, taking her hand in his and feeling her pulse.

"You're going to go into shock if you keep breathing like that. Take a deep breath and count to three, then exhale," he said.

"Do you know what to do? We should get Doctor Yoder, or Sylvia Lloyd – she's the midwife. They'll know what to do," Jacob exclaimed, the panic evident in his voice.

"There's no time for that. Like it or not, this *boppli's* coming," David replied.

"But it can't be. I didn't even know I was pregnant," Tessa wailed, and she flung her arms around Jacob, screaming in agony as a further contraction shuddered through her.

"Not everyone knows, and it looks like it's premature. Try not to panic, keep breathing and counting to three. I need hot water and towels," David said.

Rachel could not help but be amazed at how he responded to the astonishing situation they had encountered. While everyone else panicked, David remained calm and in control. He had Jacob pull cushions from the chairs onto the floor so that Tessa could be made comfortable and held her hand as he guided her into a comfortable position, all the while explaining everything he was doing.

"Will the *boppli* be all right?" Tessa gasped.

David nodded, squeezing her hand as he took a wet cloth and mopped her brow. "Let's get through it one step at a time."

Rachel kneeled next to David, smiling reassuringly at Tessa, whose breathing was now more regulated.

Jacob was watching in silence, and Rachel wondered if he felt torn between his feelings for David and the good deed he was now performing, an act that would undoubtedly save Tessa's life.

"We'll be with you all the way," Rachel said, placing her hand on Tessa's shoulder.

"What do I do now?" Tessa gasped, looking up at David, who smiled.

"You take a deep breath and push."

Rachel had never prayed as hard as she did now, but she knew that her friend was in danger and the next few minutes could take two lives or deliver one.

# CHAPTER TWELVE

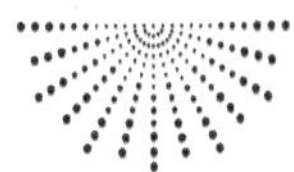

It took a surprisingly short amount of time to deliver the *boppli*. Jacob brought towels and hot water, and Rachel stayed at Tessa's side, offering reassurance as she continued to push and breathe as instructed by David.

Rachel found it remarkable to see the man she had earlier despised now come into his own. He was nothing but kind and gentle, and when the *boppli* was finally born, he wrapped it in a blanket, before cutting the cord and placing the newborn in its *mamm's* arms.

"You've got a little boy, a healthy little boy, even if you didn't realize it until a few hours ago," David said.

Rachel and Jacob helped Tessa to sit up, all of their eyes full of tears of joy.

"Oh... it's a miracle. He's a miracle. But how... I don't understand. I didn't know I was pregnant, but... isn't he beautiful?" she said, smiling up at Jacob, who wiped at the tears.

"I thought I was going to lose you, Tess. Thanks be to *Gott* you're safe, he's safe, and... we've got a *boppli*, a beautiful *boppli*," he exclaimed, a smile breaking over his face as he shook his head in amazement.

David rose to his feet and made his way into the kitchen to run the tap and wash his hands. Rachel followed him, leaving Tessa and Jacob to enjoy the first precious moments of parenthood.

"You were amazing. Where did you learn to do that?" she asked.

David smiled. "You'd be surprised what you pick up. It's not that difficult, you just have to keep calm. People always lose their heads when a *boppli* comes, but stay calm, and it'll be all right. It worked, didn't it?"

Rachel nodded. But she was still curious to know how David had remained so calm – he must have assisted at a birth before. She looked at him curiously, realizing once again that there was more to him than she had assumed.

"But... you were amazing. I couldn't have done that, and I was there when my sisters were born, albeit it was a few years ago now." She laughed, remembering how she had stood in the parlor as a little girl, listening to her *mamm* telling the midwife that she was perfectly capable of giving birth without her constant interferences.

"As I said, it's just a matter of keeping calm and not being overwhelmed," he replied.

He finished running the tap and looked around him for a towel to wipe his hands.

Rachel handed him one from the drying rack and they stood for a moment in silence, as the *boppli* began to cry in Tessa's arms.

"What are you going to call him?" Rachel asked as she and David stepped out of the kitchen.

Jacob had helped Tessa up into a chair by the stove, she was cradling the *boppli* in her arms, a smile fixed permanently on her face.

"We're going to call him Adam – the firstborn," she said, glancing at Jacob, who nodded.

"Adam was my *dawdy's* name. It seemed right to remember him," he said.

"It's a lovely name, Adam Gascho, just lovely," Rachel replied.

"Adam David Gascho," Tessa said.

Rachel smiled, glancing at David, who shook his head.

"You don't need to do that…"

"You saved Tessa's life, David. I don't mind admitting I was wrong about you. We want to name him David, too," Jacob said. He rose to his feet and held out his hand for David to shake.

After they had shaken, David excused himself, telling them he needed to get back to Clearfield Farm to see to his tasks. He made no mention of having come to seek out Jacob, and Rachel, too, took the chance to leave.

"I'm so happy for you," Rachel said, still feeling the tears in her eyes. "I'll call in and see you tomorrow. You'll want Doctor Yoder to check you both over considering the circumstances. I'll let him know what's happened and he can make a house call," she said, kissing Tessa on the cheek and placing her hand gently on Adam's brow.

He stirred, wriggling in Tessa's arms, and Rachel felt the tears welling up in her eyes at the sight of something so precious before her.

"You've both been so kind," Tessa said, as Rachel and David took their leave.

Out on the porch, Rachel let out a deep breath, shaking her head at the thought of how close they had come to disaster.

"If you hadn't been there, this could all have been far worse – far, far worse," she said, catching David by the arm.

He turned to her and shook his head, brushing her hand away as he did so. She was surprised by this action, given the words they had earlier exchanged, and she looked at him curiously, even as he turned to leave.

"Are you all right?" she asked, curious as to this apparent change of heart.

"I'm fine. I'll... see you again," and before Rachel could reply, he was gone, hurrying across the garden and through the gate out onto the lane.

Rachel stood watching him, all manner of questions racing through her mind. She wanted to know what would have happened had Jacob not interrupted them, and whether the arrival of the *boppli* had stirred previously forgotten thoughts in David, even as he had dismissed his actions as those which any other man might have performed.

*"Who are you?"* she wondered, and it occurred to her that the chance of something more between them might even now have been lost.

As she made her way home, she suddenly remembered Melinda and the reason she had encountered David that morning. Her heart skipped a beat, and she looked across the fields towards Clearfield Farm, imagining disaster having already befallen her sister. As she did so, she saw Melinda coming toward her. She was skipping happily along, and she waved to Rachel, oblivious, it seemed, to the drama which had unfolded.

"I've had the most wonderful morning," she said.

Rachel stared at her in amazement. "Didn't it occur to you we might worry? I got up and found you were gone. I came out looking for you and..." she began, but her sister only laughed.

"I told *mamm* where I'd be. I told her last night after you'd gone to bed. Harley stopped by and asked me to come and stargaze with him in the orchards. I got up early and went out. Did you follow me?"

"I... well, yes, but... I thought..." Rachel began, suddenly feeling very foolish.

She had assumed the worst yet again and made a judgment without being in possession of all the facts. Just as she had misjudged David, so too, she had misjudged her sister and Harley.

"You didn't think, that's the problem, Rach. Why can't you be happy for me?" Melinda demanded.

Rachel faltered, knowing her actions had gone beyond those of a loving sister.

She had been determined to expose what she thought was the falsity of the Sawyer brothers, even as she had come to realize she had been wrong about their cousin, too. She blushed and turned away, shaking her head and trying to make an excuse.

"I... I'm sorry, all right. I hope you had a nice time," she said.

Melinda shook her head and stormed off, leaving Rachel standing in the middle of the lane, tears welling up in her eyes.

*"I was only trying to do the right thing,"* she told herself, even as she knew it had turned out to be the exact opposite.

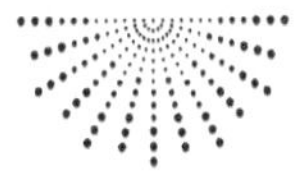

# CHAPTER THIRTEEN

Melinda had been angry with Rachel for following her that morning. There had been nothing improper in her meeting with Harley. Her *mamm* had given her wholehearted approval to the idea, and Melinda had met Harley by the gate into the orchard, bringing with him a lamp to light their way. He had led her through the long grass to a spot where they could lie on their backs and gaze up at the stars above.

It had been a warm night, and the sky was filled with so many stars as to seem like a million diamonds sparkling above. They had held hands and talked as they gazed up into the endless beauty before them. Melinda had felt happier than she had ever felt before.

But Rachel's appearance had soured those feelings and made her feel guilty for what was entirely natural. She was in love, and she wanted to spend as much time as she could in Harley's company, knowing that he, too, felt the same. He had told her as much, and when she had left, he had asked her to return the following night and gaze up at the stars once again.

She had promised she would and, making her way from Clearfield Farm, Melinda allowed herself to imagine what a lifetime in Harley's company might be like. She knew her words to Rachel had seemed harsh, but it was as if her sister was acting only through jealousy, blinded by her own rejection, and seeking to spoil the happiness of both Melinda and Sadie for her own sense of misguided revenge.

"Oh, there you are, Mel. Did you have a nice time?" Victoria asked as Melinda entered the parlor a short while later.

"It was wonderful, *Mamm.* He wants me to come back again tonight. We saw a dozen shooting stars, and the moon was so close I felt I could reach out and touch it."

Victoria smiled, pointing to a chair at the kitchen table where a simple breakfast of bread and preserves was laid out.

"I met Rachel when I was out," Melinda said, taking the seat at the table and helping herself to bread, as Victoria came to sit opposite her.

"She went out early this morning. I don't know what's gotten into her lately. She's… different. I can't quite explain it."

"She was following me. She doesn't trust Harley – or Elmer. I don't know what's gotten into her, either. Is she jealous? Upset? Angry?" Melinda shrugged her shoulders in inquiry.

She felt so confused by her sister's strange behavior. She did not like to think of Rachel being jealous, but jealousy was surely the only word for it.

"I think we've got to let her make her own mind up. She'll come around, but I agree… there's something not right. Anyway, let's not think too much about it. The important thing is that you're happy, and you've met a man who's everything you could wish for," Victoria said, smiling at Melinda, just as the bang of the porch door announced Rachel's return.

She entered the kitchen a moment later and helped herself from the pot of coffee on the side. Melinda and Victoria looked at one another and raised their eyebrows.

"Tessa had a *boppli*," Rachel said.

Melinda gasped in surprise, as did their *mamm*, who let out a cry of astonishment.

"But she wasn't pregnant."

"She was, and it's arrived. And do you know the strangest thing? It was David Knepp who delivered it…"

Melinda had listened to Rachel's story in amazement. Rachel had explained how she had met David that morning and that Jacob had appeared in a state of frenzied agitation, urging them to accompany him home.

Tessa had soon given birth to a *boppli* boy – entirely unexpectedly – and if it had not been for David, then things could have turned out a great deal worse.

It was the strangest of stories, and Melinda had been left with the impression that Rachel had changed her mind about the Sawyer cousin, even to the point of admitting she was wrong.

"I'm sorry I didn't give you a chance to explain earlier on," she had said, catching Rachel as she left the kitchen.

"It's all right, I'm sorry, too. I didn't mean to make assumptions," Rachel had replied, and the two of them had parted as friends.

It was evening now, and Melinda had spent the late afternoon napping, catching up on sleep in preparation for her night beneath the stars. She put on a warm coat and hat, for despite it being summer, the previous night had been cold, and she had shivered in the long grass of the orchard.

Harley had promised to bring a flask of hot coffee to keep them warm, and when night fell, Melinda set off across the fields in the direction of Clearfield Farm.

"There you are, I've been looking out for you," Harley said, hurrying towards her with a smile on his face.

He, too, was wearing a large overcoat and hat, a pair of gloves stuffed into his pocket, and the flask of coffee tucked under his arm.

"I've been looking forward to it all day," Melinda replied, taking his hand as he led her through the gate and into the orchard.

"Me, too. I couldn't wait to see your smile again."

Melinda blushed, swept away by thoughts of what might be between them, her mind once again wandering to marriage and the possibility of children.

"I presume David told you what happened today," she said, when the two of them had come to the spot amidst the long grass, still flattened from where they had lain the night before.

Harley looked at her with a puzzled expression and shook his head.

"I've not seen him all day. He doesn't make a point of spending time with us. He's usually off with Nancy or in his bedroom."

"So, he didn't tell you about helping with the delivery?" Melinda replied, astonished that something so important should have received no mention.

"Delivery? Do you mean leaflets? I don't know anything about him delivering something."

Melinda laughed. It seemed incredible that Harley knew nothing about what his cousin – a hero in her eyes – had done, and she proceeded to explain all about the birth and how David had saved Tessa's life. Harley listened in stunned silence, his eyes wide with astonishment.

"He did that?" he exclaimed.

Melinda nodded. "It's the truth – every bit of it. Rachel was there with him."

Harley shook his head and laughed. It seemed he was unaware of this new side to his cousin, a side which was very different from the man he thought him to be. Melinda was glad to tell him what had happened. David had saved Tessa's life, and she knew how grateful her sister was to him, and how her view of him had changed for the better.

"It's hard to believe, but... well, David knows about... that sort of thing," Harley said.

Melinda could not believe the words she was hearing; how could that be?

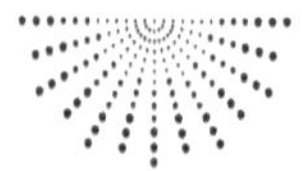

# CHAPTER FOURTEEN

Melinda looked at him in surprise, but he would say no more about it and pointed instead to the stars above them, pouring her a cup of coffee from the flask before sitting back on his elbows and gazing upwards.

"It's magnificent, it's… I've never taken the time to look up like this before," Melinda said, taking a sip of coffee and craning her neck up to gaze at the sparkling diamond dotted sky above.

"Sometimes, we need to stop and appreciate what is before us. Don't you think?"

Melinda nodded, turning to him with a smile. She was so grateful to *Gott* for allowing their paths to cross. Until she had met Harley, she had been so taken up with the possibility of a marriage that she had hardly had time to stop and look – at anything.

In his company, the pace of life seemed to slow, and there was a sense that worries over the future, or thoughts of the past, had no bearing. The moment itself was filled with possibility, and there, beneath the stars, Melinda had found happiness in the company of another person, the man she had fallen in love with.

"I do, though I'm not always that good at doing it," she replied.

He smiled at her and sat up, putting his arm around her and bringing his face close to hers. Melinda felt a shiver run through her, and she smiled back at him, slipping her hand into his, their lips meeting in a kiss.

"I want you to marry me," he whispered.

Melinda's eyes grew wide with astonishment.

She had not expected to rush so suddenly into marriage. She barely knew him, but her feelings had already overtaken her. She was in love with him, and it was clear he was in love with her. She had been raised to think of courtship as a drawn-out process, one with stages and rituals associated with it. To be faced with such a sudden question took her breath away, and she sat back, stunned by what he was asking her.

"I... isn't it too soon? There're ways of doing it, doing things right..." she stammered, but he shook his head and drew close to her again.

"Why do we have to wait? What's stopping us? I love you and you love me, don't you?"

Melinda nodded. She was so used to the conventions of courtship – to the way things were done in Faith's Creek. She imagined the horror on her *daed's* face if he could overhear their conversation now. But she was so caught up in the prospect of what he offered – the happiness that would be theirs – that she clasped his hands in hers, a smile breaking over her face.

"I do love you... but I... can we, really?" she asked, and he jumped to his feet, pulling her up with him and embracing her.

"We can get married now... well, not right now, but... we can find a bishop who'll marry us. Anyone can see we're in love. We don't have to wait. Forget convention, forget the ways it's always been done, forget what other people might think. Let's take a risk, let's get married... tomorrow."

Melinda stared at him in wide-eyed amazement, even as the idea seemed the most wonderful thing in all the world. She knew that it wasn't possible. They would have to court for a year and then the wedding would be arranged for winter, after the harvest. Occasionally it was done quicker but not for her family. Though her *mamm* wanted her daughters married she would expect a long courtship and would never allow this.

"I don't know," she said. "My *mamm*, my *daed*. We can wait a year." And yet she didn't think she could wait a year, didn't think she could bear to be without him for so long. Could they do this? Could they leave?

She knew what her family would say, and that her *mamm* would be upset not to be at the ceremony. But at that moment, none of it seemed to matter. All that mattered was the question Harley had asked her, a question she was only too happy to say *jah* to. It was what she wanted, what her secret desires had led to. This was what she had dreamed of in those foolish moments when anything seemed possible, and yet... now it was.

"I'll marry you. I know it seems sudden, but... it feels right," she said, and he smiled at her.

"Because it is right, that's why. We don't need to be held back. We can catch the bus to Bird-in-Hand and from there travel to Cedar Run, we can get married there, we'll find someone. We'll knock on every door until we find the Bishop there, and I'll get down on my knees and beg him if I have to."

"I don't think you'll need to do that, but Bishop Beiler might..." Melinda began, but Harley interrupted her.

"*Nee*, if we stay, they'll try to talk us out of it. They'll say all the things you were just thinking. They'll make us court for months, years even. Let's just do it. Let's get married and be happy."

His words were so sincere that Melinda could not help but fall under their spell. She knew it was foolish, she knew it was reckless, and she knew her family and the rest of the community would be in complete shock to hear the news. But, at that moment, none of that seemed to matter. She did not think about what might be, only about what felt right to her now, and at that moment, all she wanted was to marry Harley and be his *fraa*.

It didn't matter to her that she had yet to commit to the faith or the hurt she would cause. Logically, she knew this was wrong but young love was strong and it pulled her to him with a strength that she couldn't refuse. Once they were married they could explain.

"Then let's go, let's take off now, let's go to Cedar Run and find the Bishop, and if he says *nee*, we'll go to the next town, and the next, until we find one who says *jah*. Oh, Harley, you've made me so happy," Melinda exclaimed.

Forgetting all about the stargazing – about anything but their shared happiness – Melinda and Harley hurried out of the orchard. Melinda was exhilarated, caught up in the dream, which had now become a reality. She and Harley were to be married, and nothing mattered more than that. She was happy, happier than she had ever felt before, and she felt convinced this was *Gott's* will for her life – for both their lives.

*"I know I'm doing the right thing,"* she told herself, as the two of them slipped away into the night.

# CHAPTER FIFTEEN

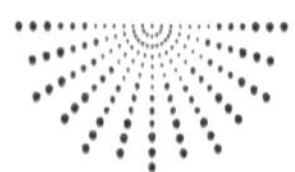

Melinda's door was firmly closed when Rachel rose the following morning, but she made no attempt to interfere, knowing how easily an argument could ensue. She would make no further comment on her sister's and Harley's courtship, and if their *mamm* was willing to let her go stargazing in the orchard at Clearfield Farm, then what business was it of hers?

She said as much to her *mamm* at breakfast that morning, even as it transpired that Melinda was yet to return.

"They're probably having breakfast together before she comes back," Victoria said.

Rachel bit her tongue, unwilling to say anything lest it causes an argument, but her heart was in her mouth and her stomach was filled with an empty hollow feeling of dread.

Her *mamm* was so caught up in the fantasy of marriage that it was hardly worth making comments to the contrary.

"I'm going to visit Tessa and the new *boppli*. Can I take some seed cake over for her?" Rachel asked, excusing herself from the table.

Abel was already out working in the smallholding at the back of the house, and Sadie was yet to get up. Victoria nodded, and Rachel was soon dressed in her shawl, and with a tin containing the cake tucked under her arm, she wished her *mamm* goodbye and hurried off along the lane in the direction of Tessa and Jacob's house. She could still not believe the remarkable events of the day before, and she kept thinking of David and how his actions had surely saved Tessa's life.

*"Everyone deserves a second chance,"* she reminded herself, knocking at the door and letting herself into the parlor.

Tessa was sitting by the stove, cradling Adam in her arms, and she looked up at Rachel and smiled. Doctor Yoder was there making notes in a small notebook, and Jacob appeared from the kitchen, as Rachel set down the tin of cake and hurried to her friend's side.

"Isn't he beautiful?" she exclaimed.

Tessa held him out for her to hold. "Doctor Yoder says he's in perfect health."

"Oh, I'm so glad to hear that – and even after… well, it's all still quite a shock, isn't it?" Rachel replied.

"A shock to us all," Doctor Yoder said, straightening up and shaking his head.

"But he is healthy, isn't he, doctor?" Jacob asked.

"In perfect health, and all things considered, that's a second miracle on top of the first. I've known women not realize they're pregnant until well into their second trimester, but this…" He shook his head.

"We've got David to thank for that," Jacob said, and Rachel looked up at him in surprise.

He had spoken so vehemently against the man, and yet there could be no doubting it was David who saved Tessa's life, and that of the *boppli*. She was glad Jacob had realized that even as she remained curious as to why the two of them should once have been so at odds.

"Why did you say those things about him the other day?" Rachel asked.

It was the missing piece of the puzzle, and she was curious to know the answer. Jacob looked embarrassed, and he glanced at Tessa, who shook her head and blushed.

"He was in love with me," she said.

Rachel stared at Tessa in amazement, and Doctor Yoder cleared his throat, excusing himself and promising to return the following day. "Any problems, come and fetch me."

They bid him goodbye, and Rachel turned to Tessa, eager to learn more about this extraordinary revelation.

"I didn't realize you knew him."

"Back in Philadelphia, on my *rumspringa*. David was there, too. We..." she began, but Jacob interrupted her.

"It's in the past. I misjudged him, though. I should've been more charitable." He raised his hands and he shook his head.

Rachel understood perfectly now, though she was surprised at Tessa for never having mentioned her association with David. But it was clear to her that once again, a jealous streak had caused division. Jealousy was truly an awful smear, one which could fester in the wounds of emotional fallout.

"Well, I think he's proved himself different from how you thought," Rachel said.

Jacob nodded. "I'm sorry if I... made you think badly of him."

"But why didn't the two of you...?" Rachel began, just as Adam began to cry.

"That sister of his... don't get me started on her. Nancy, she's nothing but trouble," Tessa replied, as she rose to her feet, cradling Adam in her arms.

Rachel made her excuses to leave.

She knew the truth now, the truth as to why Jacob should have spoken so vehemently against David, and why Tessa had defended him. There was no doubt in Rachel's mind that Tessa loved Jacob with all her heart, but to learn once again there was more to David than she had previously believed was a thought on which she dwelled.

*"He only fell in love,"* she told herself, and there was something about this realization that made her want to seek out David and talk with him again.

Instead of making her way home, she took the lane at the crossroads in the direction of Clearfield Farm, hoping for a chance to set things straight and the opportunity to mend her bridges with David...

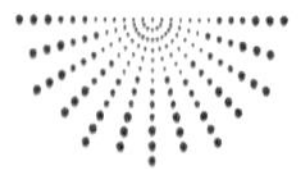

# CHAPTER SIXTEEN

Rachel found David in the orchard at Clearfield Farm. He was sitting under one of the trees, lost in thought, and he looked up at her in surprise as she approached.

"I thought I'd find you here. I just visited Tess and the baby. He's doing so well. Doctor Yoder says he's going to be fine," she said, and he nodded as she came to sit down next to him.

"It's where I live," he replied, plucking at a tuft of grass.

He seemed distracted, caught up in his own thoughts, but Rachel was determined to get him to talk. She knew everything now, and she wanted him to know she no longer had any doubts about him.

"I know about you and Tessa," she continued.

He turned to her with an angry gaze, suddenly animated by the challenge of her words. "Is that so? And what does it matter now?"

"I'm sorry I thought badly of you. It was Jacob who put those thoughts into my mind and I understand why now. I didn't mean to feel like that... well, I couldn't help it. It was... foolish," she said, willing to admit her own faults if it would bring David back onside.

She was surprised by the force of her feelings for him. It was a mixture of guilt and genuine liking. He was not the man he was made out to be, and she had seen his true character shining forth in his actions with Tessa and the *boppli*. A lesser man would have walked away and not risked something going wrong.

"That's why I told you not to listen to him. I loved Tessa, and... well, it was Nancy who put a stop to it. I shouldn't have listened to her. When I saw Tessa, and how happy she was with Jacob, it made me terribly sad. That could've been me, I could've had that life. But she found a new love easily enough, maybe she didn't ever love me, maybe it was all one-sided..." his words trailed off.

Rachel reached out her hand and slipped it into his, squeezing it, even as he shook his head sadly. "Didn't you fight for her?" she asked.

It seemed that, despite his strong words, David had done little to resist his sister's ultimatum. He could have fought for Tessa and made his sister realize how much he loved her. But instead, he had let her go, and to Rachel, that was a sign that true love had still eluded him.

"I... no, I didn't. Maybe I wasn't meant to," he replied.

They sat in silence for a moment, but all of a sudden, David looked up at Rachel with a searching gaze. Their eyes met, and suddenly, he reached out and put his arms around her, drawing her into an embrace. This sudden change surprised her, but the sensation was not unpleasant. He held her for a moment, his face pressed into her shoulder, and when he looked up, she was astonished to see tears in his eyes.

"What... what is it you want?" she asked, and he sighed, swallowing back his emotions, and shaking his head.

"I've not known the answer to that in a long time. But... meeting you... I don't know, it's changed me. This place has changed me."

"Your sister won't like it," Rachel replied.

She knew Nancy was the thorn in David's side, and she was certain that his sister had systematically attempted to alienate him from any woman who might catch his eye. Her reasons were no doubt complicated, but to stand in the way of her brother's happiness was wrong, and Rachel was not about to be cast aside based merely on the opinions of another woman. Once again, it was a judgment that stood in the way, and Rachel was determined for truth, rather than opinion, to win the day.

"She warned me..." David began, but Rachel shook her head and pulled back from his embrace.

"She warned you about Tessa, too, didn't she?"

David nodded. "Maybe I... maybe she was wrong," and to Rachel's surprise, and to her delight, he leaned forward and kissed her.

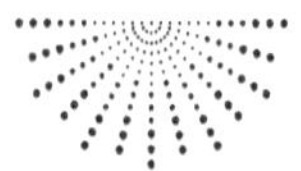

# CHAPTER SEVENTEEN

As their lips parted, David let out a sigh. It was as though he was letting go of the past and embracing a different future. Rachel smiled at him and slipped both her hands into his.

"Does this mean we've put things behind us?" she asked.

He chuckled. "I think so – I hope so, but… oh, I know what Nancy will say."

Rachel was tired of hearing about David's sister. She had barely exchanged two words with her at the games night, and since then she had kept herself to herself, but her influence was clear, and Rachel felt angry that David's chances of happiness should have been so influenced by his sister.

"Why does she have such a hold over you?" she asked.

"It's... complicated. When we lost our parents, she was so angry. I don't know how she coped, but she supported me, and I suppose... I feel I owe her something."

Rachel's heart went out to him. He had had a difficult past, even if it was still one she did not fully understand. Breaking from that past would not be easy, but David could not live in his sister's shadow forever, or allow her whims to dictate his feelings.

"But what do you want?" she asked.

David's eyes grew wide and fearful, as though he were afraid to admit it. "I... I want you, Rachel. You're all I want. I tried not to think about it, but from the moment I set eyes on you, those feelings were there. I know I've behaved badly, and I've got a funny way of showing my feelings. But I promise you, it's how I feel."

There was a sincerity in his voice, and Rachel knew he was telling the truth, even if he had a strange way of showing it.

"If you're willing to take the chance, then I am, too," she said, their hands still joined as David leaned forward to kiss her again.

Rachel felt a sense of peace coming over her, the jealousy of the past melting away. She could think of nothing but how happy she was at that moment, and as their lips parted, she smiled at him, rising to her feet and pulling him up into her embrace.

"Do you really mean that?" he asked, and she nodded.

"I saw how you helped Tessa the other day. It was magnificent. You were so calm... you saved her life. I can't thank you enough for that, but it's not only that. I was wrong about you. I judged you before I knew you, and I think you judged me, too. I'm not interested in your money – you could be a pauper for all I care. It's what's in here that counts." She placed her hand on his chest and smiled at him.

He smiled back, a look of relief coming over his face, and he kissed her on the forehead, holding her for a moment before looking down at her with a resolute expression.

"If we're going to do things properly, we should tell your *mamm* and *daed*, we should tell them we're getting married," he said, taking her hand in his and bringing it to his lips.

Rachel nodded. She knew her *mamm* would be pleased – even if she would be surprised at Rachel's change of heart. Her sisters, too, would be excited to hear the news, though they would almost certainly have something to say about Rachel's previous attitude towards their own choices. She could hear Sadie passing comments on "a change of heart." But none of that really mattered, all that mattered was that she and David had cast their differences aside for the sake of the happiness which each deserved and now, hand in hand, they made their way from the orchard and hurried down the lane from Clearfield Farm to share their joy with Rachel's family.

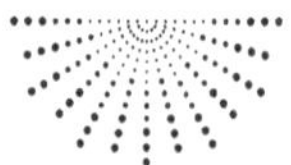

# CHAPTER EIGHTEEN

"**M**elinda is that you, thank goodness... oh," Abel said, appearing in the parlor as Rachel and David entered the house a short while later.

"What's happened?" Rachel asked as Victoria came in from the kitchen, followed by Sadie.

They were both looking anxious, even as they stared in surprise at Rachel and David hand in hand.

"It's Mel, she's gone missing... she's gone off with Harley. Elmer and Iddo have gone looking for them, but... we think they've eloped," Sadie replied, and Victoria pulled out a handkerchief and dabbed at her eyes.

"Oh, it's too awful. Why did she have to do that? Didn't she realize I'd want to be there? My own daughter getting married, and I'm not even there to witness it."

Rachel glanced at David, who shook his head as he removed his hat.

"I worried something like this would happen," he whispered.

"Do you know for certain they've gone?" Rachel asked.

She was not about to say "I told you so," but it was hardly surprising given Melinda's recent behavior. Rachel knew what her *daed* would be thinking – he would be worrying about a scandal and praying that the two youngsters had had the sense to marry, even if it was not in the spirit which her *mamm* would have wanted.

"It was Elmer who told us. He saw them slipping away in the night," Sadie replied, even as their *mamm* slumped down into a chair by the stove, dabbing at the tears rolling down her cheeks.

"Oh... my poor nerves, my poor daughter, my... but what's all this?" she asked, as though she had suddenly realized the strangeness of the sight before her.

Rachel glanced at David, the two of them smiling at one another.

"We've got some happy news, *Mamm*. With your permission," her eyes flicked to her *daed* too, "We're getting married."

Her words took a moment to sink in, her *mamm's* eyes growing wide before she gave a shriek of delight, leaping to her feet and rushing to embrace them. It seemed as though all thoughts of Melinda's disappearance had melted away, replaced by the ecstatic cry of a woman whose sole hope in life was to see her daughters married. She stood back, looking at them both, shaking her head as tears rolled down her cheeks.

"Oh, Rachel, how happy you've made me. Did you hear that Abel, Rachel's getting married!"

There was no chance that Abel had not heard the news, but the look on his face was more reserved, skeptical, even, and his eyes narrowed, even as David stepped forward and cleared his throat.

"Sir, I want to promise you I'll take good care of your daughter. We've had a rocky start, but... well, we've worked those differences out. I love her, and I believe she feels the same."

"I do," Rachel said, but her *daed* still looked concerned.

Rachel knew how hard it was for him to accept that his daughters were growing up. He would have kept them all wrapped in cotton wool, even as it was only right for them to forget a future for themselves. He shook his head, glancing at Victoria, who was dancing for joy with Sadie, who looked thoroughly bemused.

"Does that mean you won't pass comments on Elmer and me, Rach?" she asked, and Rachel nodded.

"Let's just be happy for one another," she replied, just as a knock came at the door.

"That might be news of Melinda," Abel said, and he hurried to open the door, finding Iddo and Elmer standing on the porch outside.

"No news, I'm afraid. They caught a bus somewhere, but no one knows where. I don't think we'll find them before..." Iddo said, stepping into the house, as Abel gave a groan of despair.

"Your son's got a lot to answer for."

"My son? He's a good man, he'll not hurt her," Iddo replied.

He was a tall, powerful man, with fiery red hair and a bushy beard, but despite his words, he still looked worried, as Abel turned on him angrily.

"Won't hurt her? He'll ruin her if he doesn't marry her," he exclaimed, banging his fist down on the parlor table.

"It takes two to tango, it's not just Harley…" Iddo began, raising his voice, but it was David who stepped between them.

"They're in love with one another. It's not a crime, is it? I don't think Harley's going to do anything to wrong Melinda, he's a good man, and I don't think Melinda led him astray, either," he said, glancing back at Rachel, who smiled at him.

She felt proud of him for intervening. Further proof, if any were needed, that David was a good man with a good heart. But her *daed* only scowled, and he pointed angrily at David, his face flushed with emotion.

"Good like you, is he?" he exclaimed.

"*Daed,* that's enough…" Rachel said, angry at him for speaking to David in such a way.

But David remained calm, and he nodded, holding out his hands in a gesture of humility.

"I know I've not been perfect. I've got a past, just like everyone else. But I promise you, sir, I'm in love with your daughter, and if Harley feels even a tenth of what I feel for Rachel towards Melinda, then she's in safe hands."

His words stopped Abel dead in his tracks, and he shook his head, muttering something under his breath. But Rachel could only feel proud of David for what he had done, and now he took her hand in his, smiling at her as he leaned forward to kiss her on the cheek.

"I'll marry you a thousand times," she whispered

"As soon as possible, I hope," he replied.

"As soon as possible," Victoria said, "You should have a proper courtship, you're the oldest so a few months will do, but it must look proper." The smile slipped off her face for a moment, but she clapped her hands together and put a smile back on her face, as she turned to Iddo, who was standing silently in the corner. "We'll join the branches of these two families soon enough, and I'm sure Harley will do the right thing by Melinda, just as Elmer and Sadie will do, too."

Rachel could see the conflict on her *mamm's* face. The worry, the fear, and the joy. How she hoped her sister was safe, but for now there was nothing she could do to help. She had to do the hardest thing, to wait and to have faith that all would be well.

# CHAPTER NINETEEN

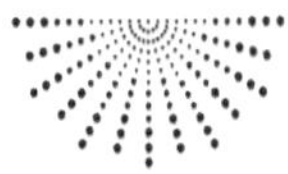

There was much by way of congratulation between them all, even if the question of Melinda and Harley's disappearance still hung heavily in the air. Abel remained surly, but he offered his congratulations to her and David, shaking Iddo's hand and apologizing for his moment of anger.

"We'll find them, I promise," Iddo assured him.

"We certainly will. I'm not having my daughter wed a man without her *mamm* there to see it. I've waited too long for this moment. Goodness, me, it's like waiting for a bus – you stand forever at the stop, and then two come along at once. Maybe three," Victoria said, glancing over at where Sadie and Elmer were sitting together in the corner of the parlor.

Rachel caught David's eye, and the two of them excused themselves, stepping out onto the porch and sitting on the swing chair. It was a beautiful day, and the sun was warm on their faces. David put his arm around Rachel, and she rested her head on his shoulder, enjoying a moment of peace after the excitement of their return that morning.

"What do you think they've done? Mel and Harley, I mean," she asked.

She was certain her sister would not have done something foolish, even if love could make a person do strange things. Her sister was sensible, and she would not have eloped so readily if she had not considered the consequences.

"I suppose they've done what they thought was right. My cousin's not a bad man, a bit headstrong, perhaps, but he's still young – we all are."

"I'm sure we'll find out soon enough. They'll come back. Mel's a home bird. She won't want to hurt *mamm* and *daed*, even if she does get married without them there."

It seemed strange to think of her and her sisters at such a stage. It did not seem long since they were *kinner*, and now each of them was forging a new identity for themselves – independent of what had gone before.

"Then there's nothing to worry about. Let's think about us, instead," David said.

Rachel liked that idea. She had resigned herself too readily to judgment, and now, when that judgment proved false, life lay before her in a happy possibility.

"And you're sure you want this?" she asked, knowing the obstacles they still had to overcome, not least of which was David's sister, Nancy, who was bound to object to the proposal.

"I know I want it. I don't care what other people say. I'll talk to Nancy, I'll make her understand."

"She shouldn't keep you from love. She did it once. You can't let her do it again," Rachel replied.

He threaded his fingers through hers, smiling at her as he rested his forehead against hers.

"She won't keep me from love. It wasn't right before, with Tess, I mean, but this... I can't imagine anything feeling righter than this. I know I've behaved badly, Rach, but you've given me a second chance, and I'll always be grateful for that."

"It's a fresh start for us both. We've each got the chance of something new. It's an adventure, don't you think?"

Rachel was excited about the future, a future very different from anything she had expected. She had fallen in love, entirely unexpectedly, but she trusted *Gott* had a plan for her, a plan which was working its purpose out in front of her – for them both. She rested her head on his shoulder, leaning into him as they gazed out across the cornfields. She felt safe in his arms and assured of a future that would bring with it only happiness for them both.

"It's the greatest adventure I could imagine. I've not felt this happy since... well, I don't think I've ever felt so happy. It just feels right, Rach, that's all I can say," he replied.

And that was all he needed to say. There was no need for further apologies, no need for further explanations. They had one another, and that was all that mattered.

* * *

If you enjoyed this book grab Melinda's Story .

123

Faith's Creek Pennsylvania

The wind lifted the ties of Emma's kapp and let them drift across her face. The breeze was nice, refreshing, and gave her a sense of freedom as did the open view before her. There was still a chill in the air and spring was yet to bring the hedges to life, but she loved this time of year.

Behind her was the center of Faith's Creek and she could still smell the enticing smells from the bakery. To her side was a cup of coffee and a raspberry and white chocolate muffin nibbled on but almost forgotten. In front of her was the widest part of the creek, or river, that the district was famous for. The sky above was blue, the blue so deep and perfect it made you feel small. It gave you a sense of the wonder of *Gott's* world, of the magnificence in the smallest things that could be taken for granted if you let them pass. The occasional cloud drifted across in front of her. They seemed lazy and indulgent, not quite as fluffy as the cumulus clouds of summer but still, they lifted her spirits. What would it be like to fly high like a cloud?

Emma chuckled, her sister Susan would consider such thoughts wasteful, "How will that get you a husband?" She could almost hear the stern tone in her voice. Lifting her paintbrush she let it slide across the paper and as if by magic the cloud was now immortalized in front of her.

Normally when she painted, she liked to work somewhere more remote. Tonight she only had time to walk here if she was to get any painting done. She had left her work in the clothing factory, ridden her bike back to Faith's Creek, and grabbed a sandwich and two muffins before sitting down to paint. Maybe two was too many, what would Susan say? That reminded her of the muffin and she lifted it and took a bite but her eyes were pulled back to the scene and how best to bring it to life on the paper before her.

The other side of the creek was pastureland and grazing on it were two large Belgian draft horses. The animals seemed to capture the sunlight and it enhanced the dapples on their chestnut coats and made their flaxen manes and tails shine.

It was Emma's second day on this painting and even though the horses had moved she had already penciled them in. All she needed to do now was capture the magnificence and the glory that embodied the horse's spirit. Holding her breath, she dipped her brush into the water and then back to the pallet, picking both orange and brown she mixed them together and delicately applied them to the paper. It was perfect, the brush glided from her hands bringing the horses to life.

Emma took another bite of the muffin as she studied the horses and their muscles. She had it, and still with the muffin in her left hand, she bent back to the painting.

Every now and then, she could hear voices behind her but one particular voice made her brush freeze above the paper. It was Amity Wayne. Emma bit back a groan. Amity was well known as a bitter old woman, a gossip, and someone who liked to pull others down.

"No wonder she's so fat," Amity said not caring that her voice carried.

Emma could not see who she was talking to and whoever it was, they were good enough to keep their reply to a whisper.

"Mark my words," Amity said again, "I don't think it's right. It goes against the Ordnung. I shall be talking to the bishop. Vanity and frivolity that's all it is, there should be no vanity in our district."

"I agree with you," another voice said.

The brush was shaking in Emma's hand. Yes, she was a little large, but surely that was the way *Gott* made her? It didn't matter. Cruel remarks had been part of her life for as long as she could remember. Emma Byler, 37 and still unmarried. 37 and hardly been courted. The woman could lose her home because she hadn't bothered to get a husband. The woman who wasted her time painting when there was work to be done. Who would even look at her! She had heard it all and even though she pretended she was strong, that she didn't care, it still cut her to the bone.

Biting back her tears she added more paint to her brush, but as she touched the paper her hand shook so badly that it smudged. The painting was ruined.

Rinsing her brush once more she wiped it clean and packed away her things. Luckily, her journey home would be in the opposite direction to Amity. Hopefully, they wouldn't meet.

With her paints, brushes, and easel all gathered under her arms, Emma started on her walk home. Even though she knew it was silly, she couldn't help but let a tear fall. Her work in the *Englischer* factory was hard, but it kept a roof over her head, just, and gave her enough money to spend on her painting supplies. Though there had always been a few mumblings about her paintings — until her *daed's* death — no one had said it out loud. Marlin Byler was a jolly man, even after his stroke. A good man who loved his community, but would not hear a bad word about his daughters.

Emma guessed that it was fine to have a little frivolity when you were looking after a dying relative. For a moment she was angry and feelings of pity overwhelmed her. Her sisters had it so easy. They were much younger than her and yet both were married. Susan had a three-year-old, little Dan. Mary had been married a few years now but so far had no children. Sometimes that worried Emma but her sister had not spoken about it.

Emma whispered a prayer of gratitude. Even though her *mamm* had been ill since Mary, her youngest sister, was born, they had had a good life. Emma had raised the two sisters and helped her *daed* as much as she could. It left little time to court and though she had always been happy, Emma had turned a little bit to food for comfort. Caring was hard work for a young girl and yet she wouldn't have missed it for the world. The hours she had with her *mamm* were treasured.

Emma walked past a large hedge up to a crossroads, struggling to carry all of her equipment and deep in thought. *What would she do if she lost her job?* Without looking she stepped out and was so engrossed that she didn't notice the buggy trotting towards her.

"Whoa!" A deep voice called.

The sound of hooves clattering to a halt sent a shock that jolted her heart and tingled all down her arms. Emma looked up to see the horse almost on top of her. She stepped aside quickly but dropped her easel and water-color pad onto the track. For one awful moment, she thought the horse and wheels of the buggy would go straight over it. However, the buggy was expertly steered around it and pulled to a halt.

Emma dropped to her knees to gather up her supplies. Could this day get any worse?

Jesse King looked out over the horse's ears as it trotted along the country lane. Faith's Creek was everything he could've hoped for and he knew that within a short time he would have more customers than he could manage. The local Bishop, Amos Beiler had invited him here as the previous blacksmith had retired. In his Ohio community, his brothers ran their family blacksmith and Jesse, even though welcome, had been looking for a new start. It was just a few years since his parents had passed, within a few months of each other. It seemed that their love was so strong that one could not survive without the other.

Shortly after that, the woman he had been courting had left him for a better prospect. It broke his heart and left him bitter and he had not approached a woman since. Although he knew that Rebecca's Zook did not deserve his love, she had it, and though he had now left her behind, his heart was still broken. It felt like a wizened old walnut to him. Hard and impenetrable.

It was at that time that he started to wonder about leaving his home. The memories were bad enough, seeing Rebecca married to Aaron Wagler was hard, but the hardest thing was the sympathy. Although he loved his aunts and uncles and brothers and their wives they were constantly plying him with sympathy. Either that or they were offering up alternatives. Jesse was not ready to give his heart again and he wondered if he ever would be.

Over the top of the hedge, he could see a young woman walking up to the crossroads. Her head was bowed and she seemed to be carrying a heavy load, both physically and metaphorically. As the horse approached the corner he waved to her but she did not look up. A hand clutched onto his heart as he realized she hadn't seen or heard him and she walked straight out almost under the horse's hooves.

"Whoa!" he shouted, hauling on the reins and steering the horse to the side. The woman raised her head and dropped all she was carrying. Jesse pulled the horse to a halt and jumped down. How could he have been so silly? He nearly ran her over!

The woman had dropped to her knees and was busily gathering up her things. Though she was dressed in the traditional Amish garb with a kapp, a dark blue dress, and a white apron. He could see that she had dropped what looked like art supplies.

The words of Bishop Bender were harsh in his ears. "Frivolity and wasteful time will not be tolerated. Work, young man, work and prayer, that is our way." He had heard them many times in his youth when he used to sketch. That was when he realized he hadn't picked up a pencil to do anything other than work in many years.

"Here, let me help you," he said bending to his knees.

She seemed oblivious and he reached out to grab her pallet of paints and at the same time she reached out too. Their hands touched and she turned to him and he saw the most beautiful pale blue eyes he had ever seen. There was something in them that pulled at his heart, was it the deep sadness, or was it something else?

Jesse felt his cheeks color and pulled his hand away as if it was burned. This was ridiculous. He was a man of 40. There was no way a woman should make him blush but there was something about her. She was beautiful and curvy with a face that looked worried and was damp with tears when he imagined it would bring out the sunshine if she smiled.

"I'm so sorry," he said. "Let me help you."

Of course, she must be married, she was beautiful and maybe a few years younger than him. Quickly he pushed away the feeling that this meeting was meant to be and tried to help. How would it look if the first week in his new district he upset one of its members?

She nodded her head and bowed so he could not see her face. Jesse wanted to comfort her but instead, he picked up her pad. It had opened to a watercolor of a small copse of trees not far from here. Cattle grazed in front of it and a bird sat on the hedge. It was so real, so beautiful that he wanted to touch it and he knew that his jaw had dropped open. "Did you paint this?" he asked.

The woman stood up and folded her arms. "I don't need you telling me I shouldn't be wasting my time," she said and grabbed the pad before turning and walking away, her arms overloaded.

Find out if Emma must quit her painting and if she can ever find love in The Amish Landscape

135

**All my books are FREE on Kindle Unlimited**

If you love Amish Romance, the sweet, clean stories of Sarah Miller receive free stories and join me for the latest news on upcoming books here

**These are some of my reader favorites:**

The Amish Faith and Family Collection

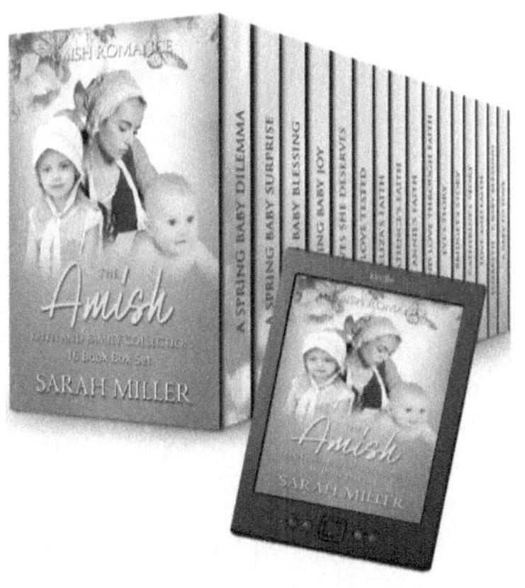

A Love Tested

A Return to Faith

15 Tales of Amish Love and Grace

Find all Sarah's books on Amazon and click the yellow follow button

+ Follow

This book is dedicated to the wonderful Amish people and the faithful life that they live.

Go in peace, my friends.

As an independent author, Sarah relies on your support. If you enjoyed this book, please leave a review on Amazon or Goodreads.

## ABOUT THE AUTHOR

Sarah Miller was born in Pennsylvania and spent her childhood close to the Amish people. Weekends were spent doing chores; quilting or eventually babysitting in the community. She grew up to love their culture and the simple lifestyle and had many Amish friends. The one thing that you can guarantee when you are near the Amish, Sarah believes is that you will feel close to God.

Many years later she married Martin who is the love of her life and moved to England. There she started to write stories about the Amish. Recently after a lot of persuasion from her best friend she has decided to publish her stories. They draw on inspiration from her relationship with the Amish and with God and she hopes you enjoy reading them as much as she did writing them. Many of the stories are based on true events but names have been changed and even though they are authentic at times artistic license has been used.

Sarah likes her stories simple and to hold a message and they help bring her closer to her faith. She currently lives in Yorkshire, England with her husband Martin and seven very spoiled chickens.

She would love to meet you on Facebook at https://www.facebook.com/SarahMillerBooks

Sarah hopes her stories will both entertain and inspire and she wishes that you go with God.